Cecile's home and property were surrounded by sheriff's deputies and forensics personnel.

Josh was one of the first to arrive. He found her on the couch, looking more fragile than he'd ever seen her before.

"What happened?" He resisted the urge to pull her into an embrace.

"A man broke into my house. He grabbed me from behind, but I managed to fight him off."

Josh glanced at the trail of blood. She'd connected with the assailant.

"I elbowed him. Think I broke his nose. He ran after that—didn't even take his stuff with him." She gestured over to the counter.

As proud as he was that she'd successfully defended herself, the pride didn't ease his panic at the sight of the shower curtain and clothesline. He didn't know if this had anything to do with the case—but the restraints the assailant left behind suggested it did. They might have just caught a break, but at what expense?

Virginia Vaughan is a born-and-raised Mississippi girl. She is blessed to come from a large Southern family, and her fondest memories include listening to stories recounted around the dinner table. She was a lover of books from a young age, devouring tales of romance, danger and love. She soon started writing them herself. You can connect with Virginia through her website, virginiavaughanonline.com, or through the publisher.

Books by Virginia Vaughan

Love Inspired Suspense

Cowboy Lawmen

Texas Twin Abduction
Texas Holiday Hideout
Texas Target Standoff
Texas Baby Cover-Up
Texas Killer Connection
Texas Buried Secrets

Covert Operatives

Cold Case Cover-Up
Deadly Christmas Duty
Risky Return
Killer Insight

Visit the Author Profile page at LoveInspired.com for more titles.

TEXAS
BURIED SECRETS

VIRGINIA VAUGHAN

LOVE INSPIRED SUSPENSE
INSPIRATIONAL ROMANCE

LOVE INSPIRED® SUSPENSE
INSPIRATIONAL ROMANCE

ISBN-13: 978-1-335-58787-9

Recycling programs
for this product may
not exist in your area.

Texas Buried Secrets

For questions and comments about the quality of this book, please contact us
at CustomerService@Harlequin.com.

Love Inspired
22 Adelaide St. West, 41st Floor
Toronto, Ontario M5H 4E3, Canada
www.LoveInspired.com

Printed in U.S.A.

Be careful for nothing; but in every thing by prayer and supplication with thanksgiving let your requests be made known unto God. And the peace of God, which passeth all understanding, shall keep your hearts and minds through Christ Jesus.

—*Philippians* 4:6-7

For Izzy. May the love of reading blossom in you.

ONE

Flashing blue lights alerted Deputy Cecile Richardson that she was in the right place. Six law enforcement vehicles blocked the road and the crime scene van was already present. Her headlights captured uniformed figures hurrying around to secure the area. She pulled her pickup to the side of the road and shifted into Park. Dread filled her at what she was about to face. A dead body. Another woman found murdered in her county.

It had taken her an hour after receiving the call to make it to the scene. She'd been out on her horse Sunflower, exploring the caves on the Henderson Ranch for her missing friend Erica—just as she did most days she was off duty. By the time she'd gotten Sunflower back to the stable, then showered and changed, darkness had set in.

Rain pelted her windshield, so she slipped

on her hat and rain jacket as she got out of the pickup. She looked around, pausing for a beat when she spotted Josh Avery's truck. The sheriff hardly ever showed up at crime scenes. This one must be something special.

She slipped beneath the crime scene tape and braced herself. The responding deputies had set up a trail through the woods with lamps. Their light broke through enough to illuminate the route, but the contrast only deepened the darkness of the surrounding area. This site was definitely off the beaten path. Deep into the woods. Not much traffic on the main road. No streetlights. No houses in sight. In other words, no one to come across a body for a long, long time. At least, that had to have been the killer's plan.

A tent had been set up over the area to protect the scene from the downpour. She spotted two people from the forensics team in their white coveralls collecting evidence, and a rectangular area of ground had been cordoned off with even more crime scene tape.

Josh stood on the other side of the tape. Rain pelted his cowboy hat and rain slicker but he seemed oblivious to the weather as he stared at the patch of overturned dirt. A grave. Her gut clenched and she braced herself. Examining a body was never pleasant but it was a necessary step.

Josh turned to her as she approached the site. His usually bright blue eyes were weary and his jaw and shoulders looked rigid and tense.

"What do we have?" she asked him.

"See for yourself."

She glanced over a mound of dirt to find a shallow grave. Inside, a battered plastic tarp held skeletal remains. Some clothing remained but not much. A bunch of long blond hair was still attached to the skull. However, the most prominent feature was the way the arms were positioned behind her. There was what looked like binding near the hands.

Their victim had been tied up, murdered, then dumped in a shallow grave. The hair and clothing that remained indicated their body was female.

Now she understood why Josh was on the scene. That made the remains of three murdered women found in their jurisdiction in the past five years. "Who found it?"

"A group of kids on their ATVs." He pointed to four boys huddled around another tent that had been set up away from the scene. Now that she looked, she spotted the ruts in the ground made by their off-road vehicles. "They were out mud riding. One of them overturned his ATV. As he was getting back up, he stumbled across the grave. Noticed part of the tarp sticking out, became curious and tried to unearth it. That's when they found the bones."

The dirt was freshly overturned but the body had decomposed to the point that they would need dental records or DNA to identify it. This was not a recent kill.

"This grave is too shallow for this to have been her original burial ground. If she had been this close to the surface, animals would have gotten ahold of this site and scattered her remains long before she could decompose to this extent." Had the kids found a bone or two, it would have made more sense, but this body appeared to be intact. Nothing looked bothered other than the fresh dirt.

"That was my thinking, too." Josh knelt. "And look at the dirt. This is a fresh grave. I would estimate she's only been here a week at most."

"Which means she was buried somewhere else first." They were on the same page in their thinking. "Someone moved her. Why would they do that?"

"Fear of being found out? Maybe Forensics

can uncover something that will give us some clues about where she was buried previously."

"Wherever it was, she had to have been buried deep—or in a spot that was well protected from animal access. These remains look to be intact. No animal pillage." That begged the question of why someone would dig up a well-concealed body and rebury it in a shallow grave, making its discovery all the more likely. The killer—statistically likely to be a male, though they couldn't be absolutely certain about that—had done his best to hide her off the main road, which indicated he didn't want her found, but he apparently hadn't wanted to go through the hassle of digging deep enough to keep her remains undiscovered. This killer's behavior so far was all over the place.

Zeke Tyler, another deputy and Josh's brother-in-law, approached them, his face drawn into a frown. "Sheriff, the news vans just arrived. They want a statement about the discovery."

Cecile wasn't at all surprised when Josh's sigh indicated that was the last thing he wanted to deal with.

Despite being sheriff, he hadn't had a good relationship with the local news media ever since his wife's murder eight years ago. He'd never officially been considered a suspect in her case, yet the media refused to give up the idea that he was somehow involved, and questions about the unresolved case always came up. She couldn't blame him for not being friendly toward them. Yet, the sheriff's office needed to remain on good terms with the local press. They might need their help in getting information out to the public about this case.

Cecile spoke up. "I'll talk to them."

Relief flooded his face and he nodded his thanks. "I'm heading back to the office. I want to pull those other cases and have another look at them. Maybe there's something we overlooked that will give us insight into what happened to this woman. You stay here and oversee the scene. Make sure everything gets done properly. If this case is related to our other victims, I want to be ready to act the moment the medical examiner's findings come in."

She touched his arm—then second-guessed herself and pulled her hand away. Even in the pouring rain and at a crime scene, she had the urge to comfort him, but she couldn't be sure her touch would be welcomed. They'd been friends for years, close friends, but that had all changed in a moment when they'd shared a kiss. They hadn't spoken of it since that night but she, at least, certainly hadn't forgotten it. On the contrary, she still felt the weight of it weeks later. They'd tiptoed around one another, hesitant to risk their friendship on a romance that might not last. But at times like this, when she saw the tension flowing off him, she wished she felt at ease enough to offer him comfort.

His blue eyes—an Avery family trait—stared down at her with grief and sadness filling them. He'd never told her so but she suspected he saw his wife Haley's face in each murder victim. She'd been killed in their cabin on his family's ranch, back when Josh's father had been sheriff and Josh had been one of his deputies. Despite their best efforts, Haley's killer had never been found. Knowing someone was out there killing women under his protection had to be a heavy burden to bear.

But they were both professionals and they had a job to do. A murdered woman had been found in their county. She deserved justice, her family deserved answers, and the community deserved to know that the killer had been found and held accountable. For Cecile, that meant collecting every piece of evidence and confirming they didn't miss anything. It could be the difference between finding a killer or letting a murderer continue to roam free.

The cold case of Cecile's friend Erica would have to go on the back burner for now since she had an active one to work. She watched Josh walk to his SUV and drive away before she turned to the news cameras lined up and gave a brief statement. "We at the Courtland County Sheriff's Office can confirm that female remains have been uncovered. The cause of death will have to be determined by the medical examiner's office but I can say we do suspect foul play."

Dirk Wilson, a local TV newscaster, shoved a microphone at her. "This makes three female murder victims in the past five years. Does the sheriff's office believe there's a serial killer in Courtland County?"

Leave it to Dirk Wilson to toss out the word serial killer to further his story and start a public panic. They didn't know for certain yet if this victim was connected to the others and to imply that she was was irresponsible on his part.

"We haven't confirmed that. I can say we are working diligently to find the person or persons who committed these terrible crimes and bring them to justice." She stared into the camera, doing her best to relay confidence. "Rest assured, the killer will not continue to prey on women in my county, not on my watch."

She thanked the press, then returned to the grave site.

Mud sloughed under her feet. She was glad she'd worn her boots. They would be caked with mud by the time she got home tonight but that couldn't be helped.

It was going to be a long night.

Josh returned to the sheriff's office, parked and walked inside. They usually had a skeleton crew working at night, most of that consisting of deputies who were usually out patrolling. However, tonight, nearly everyone on staff was at the crime scene except Deputy Marla Kemp, who was also the dispatcher, and Deputy Chase Michaels, who guarded the few prisoners they had in custody in the jail.

Josh approached Marla. "Any calls tonight?"

"Not anything urgent, boss. It's been a quiet night so far."

"Let's hope it stays that way."

He headed toward his office. If he needed to call deputies from the crime scene to handle other incidents, he would, but he preferred to have everyone on-site for as long as possible. That way, Cecile could have whatever help she needed to clear the scene and gather every piece of evidence they could find before the rain washed it away.

She kept him updated, texting him when the coroner arrived and transported the body to the medical examiner's office. He quickly fired off an email asking the ME to place a rush on examining the body. Little was left for a complete autopsy but he wanted to know whatever findings there were as soon as possible.

After sending the email, he walked to the file room and located the boxes containing the case files for the other two unsolved murders they believed were connected. He carried them to his office and dug through them. They had two female victims on file whose cases remained unsolved and shared similarities. He'd noted those same similarities in this most recent victim. Three murdered women for whom justice had not been realized.

He opened the first box and read the file.

Rhonda Carlisle. Twenty-nine years old. Her body had been found dumped in a wooded area just like their most recently discovered victim. He pulled out the photographs and noted the way her hands had been bound behind her. She'd also been wrapped up, in her case in a plastic shower curtain. Two more similarities between her and the newest victim.

He opened the second file. Twenty-four-year-old Allison Fuller. Found in a pasture three miles from her home, wrapped in a shower curtain. Her hands had also been bound behind her.

So far, they had found no connections between the lives of the two women. They'd moved in different circles. Allison, home on break from graduate school, had associated with the younger crowds. Her family had been affluent while Rhonda's family had been blue collar. Rhonda had been working as a waitress at a local diner when she was killed.

Cecile kept detailed records on both cases that Josh had gone over again and again. Neither of them had been able to establish anything common to both women. They'd gone to different churches, different schools, and lived very different lives. He and Cecile didn't even know for certain that they'd been killed by the same person, although the physical evidence seemed to suggest it. Finding another victim with obvious similarities opened up a direction he'd prayed he wouldn't have to explore.

He closed the files and placed them back into their evidence boxes. He stood and rubbed his face as he walked around to his desk. His wife Haley's image smiled at him from her photograph on his desk. He picked it up and traced his finger over her outline. He couldn't help remembering other images of her that filled their own file in a box in storage, images that devastated him. He'd forced himself to look at them more than once after her case had gone cold. His father had prevented him from getting directly involved in the initial investigation, but once it was obvious her murder wasn't going to be solved and Josh had taken over as sheriff, he'd bitten back his own dread and pulled the case.

It had sickened him seeing her that way. And it had hurt, like a punch in his gut. Like losing her all over again. But someone had to keep her memory alive. He knew that punishing himself by looking through the file didn't help anything, but at least it made him feel like he was doing something. Whatever pain it brought him, he deserved for failing to bring her killer to justice. After eight long years, the case remained unsolved, something that the local media, especially Dirk Wilson, never let him forget.

He hadn't wanted to give the files to Cecile. He'd guarded it from her, not wanting her to see the darkness in his past. She knew about Haley's murder, but she had her own dark cloud with her friend Erica and he didn't want to burden her further. But she was also the best investigator he'd ever seen. She had a knack for sniffing out the truth like a bloodhound who'd captured a scent. He depended on her professionally and personally, and he trusted her with everything—including Haley's file.

Their friendship had grown easily and he was more comfortable with Cecile than with any other person on the planet. At least, he had been until that night a few weeks earlier when he'd walked her out to her pickup. He knew he shouldn't have kissed her, but he hadn't been able to deny the draw of her any longer.

But it had been a mistake. He'd decided long ago that dating and romance weren't going to be a part of his life, not while this dark cloud of uncertainty over Haley's death hung over him. It wasn't fair to saddle anyone with that, especially not someone he cared so much about.

No. He and Cecile would have to remain friends—*just* friends. It would have to be enough for him. That and the memory of the taste of her kiss.

He prayed it would be enough for her, too.

Sundays meant church in the morning and afternoons spent at her father's ranch. Cecile usually went nonstop with a fresh murder scene to investigate, but she'd had to make an exception on this case since they were still waiting to hear back from the medical examiner and Forensics. She'd had deputies canvassing the area, but the homes near where their Jane Doe had been found were few and far between, and the folks they'd spoken to hadn't admitted to seeing or hearing anything.

Being in church usually helped to clear her mind but she was distracted today and only half heard the sermon Brother Martin preached. She spotted several members of Josh's family, including Mr. and Mrs. Avery, Bree and Lawson, and Paul and Shelby. Josh was notably missing but that wasn't all that unusual. While she knew he loved the Lord, she also knew his faith had taken a hit since his wife's murder.

She waved to the family but didn't stick around to speak with them after the service ended. Instead, she hopped into her pickup and drove to her father's small ranch. The gardens had grown over and most of the animals that had once lived here had either died or been sold off once her father became unable to care for them alone and had essentially retired from ranching. Her brothers had moved away years ago and started families and Cecile had gotten a house closer to town. They'd all tried to convince their father to move, but he was unwilling to part with his house despite being physically unable to work the land. Sunday dinner had become a family tradition that brought them all together each week.

She was the last one there as usual even though she'd come straight from church and lived closer than all of them. They didn't consider church and faith to be as important to their day-to-day lives as Cecile did. Her nieces and nephews were playing in the yard when she arrived. They ran to her and she greeted each one with a hug and kiss. She loved being an aunt and looked forward to the day when her own children would join in the fun.

She'd silenced her cell phone during church, so she took a moment to check it before heading for the house. She half hoped for a text from the medical examiner with breaking news about the body they'd discovered, but no new messages awaited her.

She joined her brothers and sisters-in-law at the picnic table. The fried chicken smelled delicious and her stomach grumbled with hunger. She hadn't eaten since lunch yesterday. She kissed her father's cheek, noting how frail and weak he looked, then she greeted everyone while she fixed herself a plate.

Her brother Charles leaned forward. "So, Cecile, I heard you found a body over in Keller Woods. Word around town is you think it's the work of a serial killer."

She should be surprised that the news had gotten around so fast, but she wasn't. Small towns were always gossip hotbeds, and her brothers weren't so removed from Courtland that they didn't hear the buzz, especially with Dirk Wilson on the job of whipping everyone into a frenzy. "It's too early to tell. We haven't even identified the body yet."

"The papers are calling the killer the East Texas Strangler," her brother continued.

She grimaced. She especially didn't like hearing that the press had named him. That would only serve to fuel this killer's ego while stirring up people's fears.

Her father put a stop to the conversation. "I don't like talk like that at the dinner table. And I certainly don't like being reminded about my CeCe being placed in dangerous situations."

"Come on, Dad. Cecile can take care of herself. She's a better shot than I am."

"Yes, I am." Cecile pointed her fork at each brother in turn. "I can outshoot any one of you."

But that argument fell on deaf ears as far as her father was concerned. She knew he regretted letting her grow up as such a tomboy. At the time, he hadn't had much choice. None of them had had an easy time of it after her mother deserted the family. Throwing Cecile in with the four boys had been easier. After she'd hit puberty, he'd tried to nudge her into a more girlie mindset, but by then, it had been too late.

He slammed an angry hand against the table and turned to her. "You're never going to find a husband if you're out shooting guns all the time."

"I don't go out shooting all the time, Dad. Outside of training, I try to never shoot my gun at all. But I'm a deputy sheriff. Carrying a gun is part of my job."

"Well, I don't like it. And look how you're dressed."

She'd chosen a pair of nice slacks and sandals to wear to church and hadn't had time to change. Her outfit was dressier than what the others were wearing, but it was still pants, so there was no way her dad was going to approve.

"Women should wear dresses," he told her. "How are you ever going to find a husband and give me grandchildren if you don't ever dress like a woman?"

One of her sisters-in-law admonished him for his attitude, but Cecile could have told her to save her breath. It wasn't anything she hadn't heard before—from her father and from others.

After an afternoon of fun with her nieces and nephews, she arrived home, kicked off her sandals and fell onto the couch. Usually, she did her best to ignore her father's comments, but tonight they bugged her. Not that she believed all her problems would be solved if she wore dresses…but the fact that she didn't have any romantic prospects—for whatever reason—was weighing on her more and more.

That probably had more to do with her developing feelings for Josh Avery than anything else. Things had been weird between them for weeks and their usually close relationship was strained. He didn't seem to notice or care that her feelings for him had changed. She thought she knew why, too. Despite kissing her, he still saw her as a friend, not as a woman with dating potential. He kept Haley's photo on his desk and it was clear he didn't have eyes for anyone else. There was nothing Cecile could do to change that.

She took a deep breath. Her relationship with Josh had never bothered her before. It certainly wasn't like she'd avoided romance because she was waiting for him to move on from Haley's memory—she knew that would never happen. No, the real reason Cecile wasn't in a relationship was because she'd never really made time for one. Her search for her best friend, Erica, had taken up a big chunk of her life. Her friend had gone missing ten years ago after a graduation party and Cecile had sworn to never let her case go cold. She'd spent the past decade searching for answers to what had happened to Erica, a decade when she otherwise could have settled down and started a family like her brothers and her friends. Work and church kept her content with her life but, more and more lately, she was feeling dissatisfied and ready for a change. She wasn't going to give up her search for Erica, but she needed something more in her life.

Chills rushed through her along with the overwhelming sensation of being watched. She tried to shake it away, but the feeling lingered. Suddenly, a noise from outside grabbed her attention. She walked to the window and peeked out, uncertain what had broken the silence of the night. She walked into her bedroom and unlocked her gun safe, pulling out her service weapon. She moved to the front door and opened it, peering outside. Everything seemed normal. Nothing was out of place and she no longer heard anything.

She stepped back inside and placed her gun on the end table. This case was really getting to her. The idea that a serial killer might be operating in their area was disconcerting. She was letting this killer get into her head. Yes, the victims had all been women around her age, but that didn't mean she had any particular reason to worry about her own safety. She'd always been able to handle herself in any situation, and her law enforcement training, as well as her expertise with guns, served her well. She wasn't the type of person to cower and hide. That just wasn't who she was.

She returned to the couch and settled back down. She was letting her imagination run wild. She turned on the television, hoping that a little background noise would help ease her tension. She was studying the photographs from the crime scene when the sound of glass breaking grabbed her attention.

She definitely hadn't imagined that.

She reached for her gun and got up, creeping down the hallway toward where the sound had come. She opened her bedroom door and scanned the room. Nothing. She moved down the hall to the back bedroom where she kept her office, including her investigation files on Erica's disappearance.

Glass littered the carpet beneath the window along with dirt and a shoe print. She tensed even more than she'd thought possible.

Someone was inside the house.

She checked the closet. Empty. She stepped

back to the hall. She raised her gun and walked back to the kitchen, bracing for a confrontation.

A figure leaped from the hall closet and knocked her weapon from her hand. She struggled against his hold instinctively before her training kicked in. She stomped down hard on his foot. When he cried out and loosened his grip on her, she spun and elbowed him in the face. He swore, taking several steps backward and bringing his hands to his face. Cecile dove to the floor for the gun she'd dropped. Relief flooded her the moment the cold grip was in her hand. She spun around, gun raised.

Her assailant was gone. A trail of blood led across the floor to the back door. Cecile rose to her feet. She couldn't let him get away. But by the time she reached the door, he was out of sight.

She grabbed her cell phone and placed a call to dispatch. "I need backup. A man broke into my house and attacked me." She glanced at the splotches of blood on the floor. "Send the forensics team, too. We've got blood from the assailant."

She ended the call, then turned and spotted something on the counter that made her tense. A roll of clothesline and a folded, plastic shower curtain. All three of the murder victims had been wrapped up in plastic with their hands bound.

Panic gripped her and she struggled to catch her breath. Had she just been assaulted by the same serial killer she was hunting? Had he come to her home knowing that she was on the case? Or had his attack been random?

She steadied herself. Either way, too bad for him. He'd just made a huge mistake in targeting her.

She had his blood on her floor, which meant she now had his DNA. If he was in their database, he was as good as captured.

Within ten minutes of her call, Cecile's home and property were surrounded by sheriff's deputies and forensics personnel.

Josh was one of the first to arrive. He found her on the couch. He'd never seen her look so fragile before. It worried him—even though her demeanor changed the moment she saw him. She slipped on her mask of confidence as she stood to face him.

"What happened?" He resisted the urge to pull her into an embrace. Not only would that be unprofessional, he didn't want to blur the lines between them anymore than they already were.

"A man broke into my house." She explained about hearing the glass breaking and then finding the broken glass and dirty shoe print. "He grabbed me from behind and knocked my gun out of my hands, but I managed to fight him off."

Josh glanced at the trail of blood. She'd connected with the assailant.

"I elbowed him. Think I broke his nose. He ran after that—didn't even take his stuff with him." She gestured over to the counter.

As proud as he was that she'd successfully defended herself, the pride didn't ease his panic at the sight of the shower curtain and clothesline. She could take care of herself, but that didn't make it any easier to accept that she'd been targeted. He didn't know if this had anything to do with the case—but the shower curtain and line the assailant left behind suggested it did. They might have just caught a break, but at what expense? He wouldn't risk Cecile's life even to catch a serial killer.

He headed into her office to examine the broken window and shoe print. His team would photograph that and try to make a match. They would get a better sample from the shoe print left outside the window. It was something. But the blood evidence was their biggest lead. If their assailant's DNA was in the system, it would lead them right to him.

A collection of photographs caught his eye as he stood and looked around the small room. The space was stuffed with information about her friend Erica's disappearance. She had an evidence board that took up nearly one wall and boxes of papers on the case. It was a case that had consumed her for ten years. He'd known of her obsession, but he hadn't realized how extensive her investigation into it had been.

He remembered when Erica had gone missing. He'd been on the job as a deputy. It had been big news in the county at the time. Erica had been a well-liked girl who had simply vanished during a graduation party one night. He'd even been at the party with Haley and seen nothing out of the ordinary.

He picked up a photograph of Erica and Cecile from the desk. The two of them had clearly been best friends, maybe even as close as sisters. He understood the desire for answers. He felt the same way about his wife's murder.

"She was beautiful, wasn't she?"

He turned to see Cecile standing in the doorway, her arms draped across her chest.

He set the framed photo down. "Yes, she was."

"We met in the fourth grade and were best friends right from the start." She picked up the photo and tears glistened in her eyes. She touched her friend's image. "I still can't believe she's gone. How could she disappear? And how could no one know even after all these years what happened to her?"

She didn't say it as a slight against the sheriff's office but her words still cut. They had a duty to the residents of their community, but despite their best efforts, killers still evaded justice and lost people went unfound. "I'm sorry, Cecile."

"I left her that night."

"When? The night of the party?"

She nodded. "We promised each other to stick together, but I left early. I walked away to—" She pressed her hand to her face before continuing. "When I came back, she was gone."

"It's not your fault."

Her eyes shone with tears as she looked up at him. "It was. I promised to stay with her and I broke that promise. Whatever happened to her, happened because of me." Her whole body seemed to tremble as she hugged the photo to her chest.

Tonight's attack must have brought up some of that emotion. It couldn't stay repressed no matter how tough she pretended to be. Everyone had a breaking point.

"I'm sorry," she told him, wiping her face. "I shouldn't be burdening you with this."

"Cecile, it's no burden. You know me better than that."

She stared up at him and his arms ached to hold her, but that wouldn't be fair. He would be taking advantage of a moment when she was vulnerable. Plus, she deserved better than a man whom the whole town suspected of killing his wife. That wasn't going away anytime soon and she already had enough going on in her life.

She placed the photo back on the desk, then wiped her face. "I'd better go clean up before someone sees me like this."

She was trying to save face. He understood that. She had an image to uphold. The younger deputies all looked up to her, and he knew she worked hard to always present herself to them as the ultimate professional. But she was also a person, a woman, and everyone needed an outlet.

"Why don't you take a day to rest and recover? The investigation will still be there when you get back. Besides, the forensics reports will take time. I'll call you if someone comes through."

"Thanks, Josh, but I'd rather work." She rubbed her arms and he spotted goose bumps on them. Her home had been invaded and that would take some time for her to come to terms with. But Cecile was a strong woman. She'd taken care of herself tonight and she could handle whatever was thrown at her.

She walked across the hall into the bathroom and shut the door. He headed outside and found a piece of wood along with a hammer and nails in her shed that he used to cover the broken window after his forensics team had collected their evidence. He sealed it up tightly. No one would be getting inside that way again. He checked the rest of the windows and then double-checked the locks. The house was as secure as he could make it for now—but that wasn't nearly as secure as he'd like. Cecile lived off the road and her closest neighbor was a quarter mile away. Anything could happen to her out here and no one would know it. He didn't like it but he couldn't exactly order her to leave.

It also begged the question, why would someone break into this house? Was it a random burglary or had the perpetrator come with an agenda?

The presence of the shower curtain and clothesline seemed to suggest she'd been deliberately targeted. Josh prayed the blood evidence would provide them with a DNA match but that would be days, maybe weeks, away. They couldn't wait that long. He'd already lost Haley to a killer.

He couldn't lose Cecile, too.

TWO

Josh was going over the weekly schedule with Cecile the next day when the phone on his desk buzzed and the receptionist's voice broke through. "Josh, Sheriff Milton is here to see you."

Cecile's eyes widened. "What does she want?"

"I phoned her last night, asking if she had any cases that match ours. I didn't expect her to show up at our door." He punched a button on the phone. "I'll be right there."

He turned back to Cecile. "We'll continue this later."

She opened the door and walked to her desk. He stepped out to meet Sheriff Milton, shook her hand and led her back to his office.

"I was expecting a phone call, Jennifer. You didn't have to come all the way here."

"I know but this is important." She removed her hat and tucked it under her arm as he closed the office door. "After your call, I looked back through our files. We have three open homicides on the books, the victims all matching the parameters you mentioned." She handed him three folders.

Josh opened the first one and saw photographs of a dead woman. He had to agree the similarities were striking, right down to the shower curtain she'd been found in. "How long has this been going on?"

"The three cases are all from the past four years. All remain unsolved. There's no obvious connection between the victims, but we suspect the cases are related based on the methods the killer used." She stood and placed her hands on her hips. "I've also spoken with Sheriffs Rounder and Mitchell. They too have unsolved homicides on their books that match ours. Are we looking at a serial killer, Josh?"

He closed the file, then leaned back in his chair. This was his worst-case scenario happening. "It sure looks that way to me." He'd heard murmurings about similar cases in neighboring jurisdictions, but each office had held back details from the press so no one had officially put them all together. Until now.

"Me, too." She walked around his office,

glancing at his photos and memorabilia on his shelves. "I came here today to suggest forming a task force to search for this killer. It'll make it easier to share information across jurisdictions."

"That's a good idea." It was just what he'd been thinking. Sharing information, sharing evidence, catching a predator.

"Your department should take the lead."

He straightened in his chair. Now, that was something he hadn't expected. Few law enforcement professionals stepped aside to let someone else be in charge, especially in a case of this magnitude.

She shrugged at his disbelieving expression. "We're short-staffed. I've got two deputies out on injury and one on maternity leave. It's taking all I have to cover my county. I don't have the manpower to head up an investigation like this out of my office. Besides, Cecile is one of the best investigators in the area. I think she should be the lead on this."

"You want Cecile to lead the task force?"

She nodded. "I do."

He couldn't deny that Cecile was more than capable. It just struck him as odd to hear someone else talking about his deputies that way.

"You should also know that I'm doing my best to lure her to my office."

That got his attention. "You offered her a job?"

"I did. I want her on my team."

He glanced out into the bullpen, where Cecile was working at her desk. He couldn't imagine this place without her. He could hardly imagine his life without her. Dread filled him as he asked the question he wasn't certain he wanted to know the answer to. "Did she accept your offer?" He choked over the knot in his throat.

She gave him an understanding smile, then shook her head. "No. Or rather, not yet. She's very loyal to you, but I'm persistent. You should watch your back. I'm not the only department who wants her on their payroll. Cecile has made quite a name for herself throughout Texas. From what I've heard, she's received several offers from all over the state plus Louisiana. She could have her choice of investigative jobs." She paused to let that sink in, then continued. "I'll have our complete files sent over to you. I can also offer two deputies to the task force."

He stood and walked her to the door. His hand shook a little but he did his best to remain composed as she stepped out. "Sounds good. We'll set up the task force in our conference room and put together a communication system to connect everyone."

She walked away and he saw her stop at Cecile's desk. Josh couldn't hear what they were saying but Cecile smiled at her and shook her hand. He didn't like it. Not one little bit. He knew Cecile was a great investigator. She'd led investigations into murder cases, abductions, drug trafficking and many more criminal cases throughout the years, including some that involved his own family members. He depended on her for her skill and insight. It bugged him to think she'd received job offers and never told him. He didn't realize they had secrets between them. Would she leave his department for bigger and better opportunities? She probably deserved more recognition and compensation than their little county could offer her, but he didn't want to lose her.

He called out and waved her to his office. She walked in and he closed the door.

"What's up? What did Sheriff Milton have to say?"

He picked up the files and handed them to her. "They have three unsolved murders that might match up to the ones we have."

Cecile's shoulders drooped. She took the files. "We are looking at a serial."

"Looks like. She wants to form a task force to cut through the jurisdictional red tape."

"I think that's a good idea."

"I'm glad to hear it, because you're leading it. You're good at your job, Cecile. Everyone knows it." She started to protest, then stopped and shifted uncomfortably from foot to foot. "She also told me she offered you a job with her department."

Her cheeks reddened and she shrugged it off. "That was a while ago. I turned her down."

"Well, apparently, she isn't taking no for an answer." He folded his arms and leaned against the desk. He didn't mean to put her on the spot but he had been kind of blindsided by Jennifer's declaration. "How come you never told me?"

"There wasn't anything to tell. I said no."

"Are there any other job offers on the table?"

"None that I'm considering. I would let you know if I had any plans of leaving. I don't. Besides, you know I'm not going anywhere as long as Erica's case is still open."

She was committed to finding out what

happened to her friend. Her commitment was admirable…but he hoped that wasn't the only thing keeping her in town.

She held up the files. "I'll get started looking through these and see how they match up against our victims."

He stood and opened the door for her. "I'll arrange to have the complete files sent over from all involved counties. Pull anyone you want to help you with this. And, Cecile, I'm available to help as well."

She nodded her understanding, then walked out.

He watched her go. A pang hit him in the gut. What would he do if he ever lost her? He couldn't imagine. He sat back down at his desk and stared at the photo of Haley. It had been eight long years since she was taken from him, murdered in the home they'd shared, her killer never found. He'd spent a good chunk of his life obsessing over her unsolved murder.

Over those same years, Cecile had become his best friend—and his feelings for her didn't stop there. But except for that one kiss, he'd kept his deeper feelings buried. Every time he thought about crossing that line into something more, Haley's face on his desk stopped him. He could never saddle Cecile with the stain he carried. Until Haley's murder was solved, his involvement would always be suspect. She deserved better than that.

So, for now, he kept that line in sight, the one he could never cross with her.

No matter how much he wanted to.

Within hours, boxes of evidence arrived at the department from neighboring counties along with at least one deputy from each county assigned to join the task force. Cecile had the boxes taken to the conference room and lined up against the wall. She organized them by jurisdiction and date of death, putting together a potential timeline for the killer. She'd pulled in three deputies from her own office to assist her and the others—Zeke, Marla and Greg Frasier. Their first goal was to weed through the cases and pull out the ones that didn't fit a pattern either through different physical evidence or behavioral patterns.

She was knee-deep in case files when she heard familiar voices and turned to find Josh with his brother Miles and his sisters-in-law, Melissa and Bree, enter the conference room. She greeted them all. She knew them each well.

"How's the planning going?" Cecile asked them, referring to the fiftieth wedding anniversary party for Josh and Miles's parents that Miles and Melissa were in town to make final preparations for.

"Good, good," Bree stated. "As you know, we've booked Jessup Farms for the event. They have that beautiful restored barn to house the party. We've also ordered the food and flowers, plus a band. Everything is in place for Saturday night."

Melissa reached out to her. "You are coming, aren't you, Cecile? We'd love to have you."

She had the invitation pinned to her refrigerator. "I wouldn't miss it." The Averys had been good to her. Cecile considered them like family and knew they felt the same way about her. She was honored to have been included in the celebration. It was difficult to imagine the kind of love that lasted for fifty years. She glanced at Josh and wondered briefly what it would be like to spend the next fifty years with this man. Her face warmed at that thought. That would never happen. Josh would never move on from Haley.

Miles stepped into the conference room and looked over the photos they'd pinned onto a bulletin board. "You really think you're dealing with a serial killer?"

"I'm more certain of it than ever. We've received files from six counties and identified ten unsolved murders that have distinct similarities. Enough similarities to believe they were all committed by the same person. We're working to connect the cases forensically."

Bree shuddered. "It's horrifying to think a serial killer has been operating in our area without anyone realizing it."

Though Cecile knew it hadn't been meant as a criticism, she couldn't help feeling a little guilty. She was known as a capable investigator. "He's been smart," she admitted. "He's spreading out his kills, crossing jurisdictions, which makes it even more difficult for any one department to identify a pattern. Now that he's on our radar and we're sharing information, I think we stand a good chance at catching him."

"I hope so," Miles stated. He turned away from the images. "We'd better go. We still have several stops to make before heading back to the ranch."

Cecile waited until the others had left to update Josh on the case. "We've identified a modus operandi for all these victims. It looks like he binds their hands and feet, strangles them, then stabs them multiple times before wrapping their bodies in a plastic shower curtain or tarp and then dumping their bodies. There have also been traces of gasoline or motor oil on some of the victims' hair and clothes. Nothing in the victims' files indicates that they'd have been in contact with those substances in their usual daily routines, so they likely came from the killer. He might have a garage or shed on his property for cars or a lawnmower or something similar. The fact that the oil is on the hair and clothes indicates that he might take his victims there before he kills them—definitely before he wraps them in a tarp. According to the timeline I'm creating, his kills are getting more frequent and his disposal method less elaborate. He's changed from burying his victims to basically dumping their bodies in shallow graves or no graves at all."

"How do you know his disposal method has changed and this isn't someone else?"

"We've managed to group together all the victims that share a certain signature." She picked up a photograph of one of the victims and pointed him to their hands. "See the way he ties them? In later cases, as he gained confidence, it looks like he brought his own binding, but in the earlier cases, he used whatever was handy—a cord from a lamp, fishing line, even one victim's apron strings to bind his victims' hands and feet. And yet even when the type of binding is different, the knots are the same. That's not a coincidence and it's not typical. It's his signature."

Instead of being glad that she'd found this many open cases to tie together, he looked sick to his stomach. She couldn't blame him. This guy had been out there operating for years without being noticed. Well, now he'd gotten their attention.

"Where are we on suspects?"

"We're still going through the files. Each case has a list of suspects personally connected to each victim, and most of them were cleared by the investigators. We're looking for patterns in each to see if the same name overlaps any of these cases."

He sighed. "Our counties may be separated by jurisdictions, but small towns means you're likely to find a lot of overlap between people that knew one or more of the victims."

"I know but it's a place to start."

"It's a good place. Keep me updated." He started to walk out, then turned back to her. "I'm glad you're coming to the anniversary party. My parents will appreciate seeing you there."

"I'm glad to go. I love your family, Josh. You know that."

She watched him go, then fell into a chair. His family had taken her in and made her feel like she belonged. And her friendship with Josh only cemented that feeling. But she couldn't stop herself from wanting more. Would Josh ever be able to move past the loss of his wife and come to see Cecile as more than a friend? Would he ever see her as a woman he wanted to build a life with?

And could she continue working so closely with him if he didn't?

Cecile parked her truck by the back fence of the Henderson Ranch and unloaded her horse from the trailer behind her truck. Sunflower was already saddled and ready to go for another few hours of searching. Cecile needed a break from going through the files of murdered women. She also needed to exercise Sunflower. And there was no point in not combining the two by using the remaining daylight to continue her search.

Cecile had spent years interviewing people and following up leads about Erica's disappearancc, but with no new leads to follow, she'd started performing her own searches. She was unlikely to find anything, but it was better than doing nothing. The graduation party Erica had vanished from had been on the adjacent property right by the fence line to Henderson Ranch. She concentrated her search efforts to several square miles in that vicinity. Ten years ago, this had been open land and Henderson hadn't had his fences up yet. This part of his property had been fenced off four years later as he pushed his cattle back…so he said. She suspected it had more to do with him wanting to curtail her exploring than anything to do with his day-to-day ranch operations. She'd spoken to several of his ranch hands who admitted he never let his cattle graze this far out.

She opened the gate and walked Sunflower inside before closing it securely again. She climbed onto Sunflower, then took out her map. There was a small section on the east side of the ranch that she hadn't searched yet. That was where she was starting today. A ridge of small caves was located there, the perfect place to potentially hide a body.

She tucked the map into her jacket and headed in that direction. This was the way she spent most of her free time and all of her days off. Some days, her search seemed endless. It had been ten long years with no clue of what had happened to her friend. She'd followed all the leads and tracked down and spoken to all the witnesses. She'd even chased a tip about a sighting of Erica all the way to Seattle, Washington, only to have that too be a dead end.

There were rumors that Erica had run away and started a new life. Cecile had investigated the possibility, but all along, she'd known that couldn't be true. Erica's life hadn't been perfect, especially after her father had died when she was in her tweens, but she'd had nothing to run away from. She'd lived with her mother. The two of them had been close. They hadn't had a lot of money, but her mother had scrimped and saved to give her daughter the ability to go away to college and they'd both been looking forward to it. Cecile and Erica had even planned to be roommates. Her friend had vanished a month before they were to leave.

Something had happened to Erica at the party that night and her body was out there somewhere in the Texas landscape waiting to be found.

At first, it had seemed like a mountainous job to search for her but Cecile had broken it down bit by bit. What else could she do? She'd followed all the leads she had. Random searching was the only option left and she would continue it until another lead in Erica's case appeared.

She hurried Sunflower toward the ridge and spotted the caves atop a rocky hill. She slid off and held her reins as they approached them. She pulled her flashlight from her saddle pack and steadied her horse. "I'll be back. Don't go anywhere," she told Sunflower before looping the reins around the branch of a sapling.

She climbed up onto the rocks until she reached the mouth of one of the caves. She clicked on her flashlight and shined it, breaking through the darkness before gathering her courage and stepping inside. The low overhead made it difficult to walk but she pressed on. The sides of the small cave were cool to the touch and the ground felt mushy beneath her feet. A sudden fear of what she might find inside rushed through her, including wild animals such as, she gulped, bats. She pushed through. They couldn't be any worse than finding a ten-year-old dead body, could they?

She searched through two of the caves without coming across anything of note but was several feet into the third cave when an odor reached her. She crinkled her nose at the familiar, unpleasant smell. Decomposition. She braced herself and covered her mouth and nose with the bandanna she wore, to muzzle the smell of death. She was close to something dead and inching nearer. Her light illuminated the floor of the cave until she spotted something several feet away. She paused, wondering if she was really ready to face this if it was her friend. But she owed it to Erica. She braced herself and kept going.

She held her light over an unrecognizable mass on the ground. She had to get a closer look, but the smell was overpowering. She took a few steps closer, held her breath and then knelt down for a closer look.

Her body relaxed and she quickly backtracked. Not Erica. Not even human, but some sort of dead animal that had crawled into this cave and died.

Once she was able to, she turned and ran toward the open mouth of the cave and into the sunlight. She wasn't sure if she was more relieved that it hadn't been her friend's remains or that she was finally free from the smell. She removed the mask and took several deep breaths of fresh air, gagging at the lingering smell in her nose. She was definitely glad to be away from that odor. But after a few more breaths, relief faded and sadness crept into its place. Finding Erica wouldn't have made her happy but it would have provided some closure.

"You're not supposed to be here."

She grabbed her gun from its holster and spun around, surprised to find Josh standing by the hill of rocks only a few feet away. She spotted his horse at the bottom, tied next to Sunflower.

He raised his hands. "Whoa, slow down. It's only me, Cecile."

She holstered her gun, irritated that he'd caught her so off guard. She'd been so relieved at not finding Erica that she hadn't been paying enough attention to her surroundings. "What are you doing here?"

"I got a call from Frank Henderson about someone trespassing on his property again. I didn't have to guess who it was, especially when I found your truck and trailer parked by the back gate. I followed your trail."

"How did he know I was here?"

"He added motion sensors to all his gates.

He knew the moment you stepped onto his property." Josh gave her an admonishing look. "Cecile, you have to stop this."

"I can't. Not until I find Erica."

"You're conducting a search with no parameters. You've got no authority and no warrant. What are you going to do if you find her? Nothing you uncover would be admissible in court."

"I have to try, Josh. My friend went missing around this area." She'd already exhausted every other lead she could in Erica's disappearance. This was all she had left to do.

He closed the distance between them and stared down at her. "I know you want to find your friend, but this isn't the way to do it. We're officers of the law. I can't keep putting Henderson off. Technically, you are trespassing."

She didn't want to have this argument with him right now. She still had several hours of daylight left. She wanted to continue searching for as long as possible—but she knew Josh wasn't going to relent on this.

The sun reflected off something on the ground. Cecile bent down and grabbed a silver necklace from the ground near the cave. As she did, a shot rang out, barely missing her head. She and Josh both reached for their guns, dropped to the ground, then scanned the area. There was no one in sight. However, several more shots sent them both scurrying down the rock hill. Josh grabbed her hand and pulled her along as the gunfire continued.

Her foot slipped and she stumbled but Josh caught her and helped her up. She wanted to know who was firing at them and why but there was no time to look around and try to find answers. They had no cover until they reached the bottom. Josh reached it first and crouched behind a boulder with his gun drawn.

"I can't see anyone. Whoever it is has to be firing from behind that tree." He pointed to a lone brush area on the other side of the hill. Thankfully, both horses were still tied and hadn't bolted. Her rifle was attached to the saddle and she spotted a rifle on Josh's horse as well, but at this distance, they wouldn't do much good.

"Let's get out of here."

She darted toward Sunflower and quickly climbed into the saddle before urging her horse into a gallop. Josh hopped onto his mount and took off, too. She didn't glance back, but after several minutes the gunfire ended.

They were nearly back to the gate, running side by side, when Josh slowed his horse down to a trot. She slowed, too, and turned to look back. No one seemed to be following them. Her heart was beating a mile a minute. Why had someone shot at them?

Josh pulled his shotgun from its holster just in case the shooter tried again, then reached for his radio and called for backup and a forensics team to meet them at Henderson's east gate. Her heart was still hammering but she stroked Sunflower's neck to settle her. The horse had had as big a fright as Cecile and she was glad to know her mare had stood up to it.

"What's that?" Josh asked, motioning to the chain still gripped in her hand.

This necklace had saved her life—if she hadn't bent down to pick it up, that first shot would have killed her. "The sun reflected off it. I reached down for it when the gunfire started." The chain held a simple silver cross. She turned it over. Nothing was engraved on it. "Someone must have lost it while exploring the caves."

"So you're not the only trespasser on Henderson's land."

She scowled at him and he gave her an amused grin. "I guess not. Who do you think was shooting at us? Henderson?"

"No, he knew I was coming out here. He wouldn't have called me if he was going to take matters into his own hands." He pulled out his phone. "Just in case, I'll give him a call while we wait for the rest of the team to arrive."

She slipped the necklace into her pocket, then slid from her horse and opened the gate, closing it again once they'd both gone through. Josh trailered his horse while Cecile did the same with Sunflower. Then she dug for an evidence bag in her truck and slipped the necklace inside. At least, it was a piece of evidence that had saved her life. At most, it might be a clue as to who had shot at them and why.

"I have no idea who would be shooting at you," Frank Henderson told Josh when he called. "I'll check with my security team but I can't imagine it was any of my guys." Henderson called the sheriff's office often to complain about trespassers on his property, but he'd hired a team of security specialists— most of them former military, from what Josh had heard—to keep his ranch secure.

Josh ended the call, feeling reasonably confident that Henderson was telling the truth and that he hadn't been behind the gunshots.

He heard vehicles approaching and turned to see Zeke and Greg arriving along with the forensics van.

He approached Cecile, who was standing by her pickup. "Henderson insists it wasn't him, and he doesn't think it was any of his men shooting at us, but he's going to check with his security team to confirm."

"Why does he need such an extensive security team anyway?"

"He claims he has a problem with poachers."

Cecile shot him a disbelieving look and Josh just shrugged. It was true that poaching wasn't much of an issue in their area, but he supposed Henderson had his reasons. And whether or not there were any poachers around, Josh couldn't deny there were trespassers on the land. Even one on his payroll.

Josh helped Zeke and another deputy unload the off-road vehicles Zeke had brought via trailer. He handed the deputy the keys to his truck and asked him to return his horse to the ranch, then leave his truck at the sheriff's office.

Cecile climbed into the utility vehicle next to him, her shoulder bumping his and the scent of her rolling over him. Even after dredging through caves and being chased on horseback, her scent was unmistakable—and nearly alluring enough to overpower him. He placed both hands on the controls. He had to keep his feelings for this woman to himself. Nothing good could come of them.

Especially since she wasn't going to be happy with him when he put his foot down about her fruitless searching expeditions. She was an officer of the law. She couldn't just trespass on someone else's land because she felt like doing so.

They rode in silence, the easy comfort of their friendship overshadowed by the wall between them that had suddenly and out of the blue been erected ever since the kiss. He didn't know how to tear it down. He wasn't sure he could.

They reached the rock hill and then past it to the small patch of trees and bushes that stood like a mini oasis. Just as Josh had noted in the heat of the moment, it was the only vantage point close enough to make those shots while still hiding the shooter.

He parked and got out. Cecile followed him while the rest of the team spread out to search for any forensic evidence that might have been left behind. The grass around the biggest tree was smashed down, an apparent sign that someone had been here recently. He knelt and studied the ruts in the tree. Someone had used it to steady their rifle.

"I don't see any evidence of shells or bullet casings," Cecile commented. "He cleaned up after himself."

"You're right, but there are tracks from what looks like an ATV or other off-road vehicle." The grass wasn't wet but it wasn't dry, either. The tracks weren't obvious, but they were there. "These tracks could have been made by anyone over the past few days, but let's mold them regardless. I'll check with Henderson's security manager and see if any of his team have been out this way recently."

He stared up at the ridge of caves. He raised his hands into an aiming motion. From here, the line of sight was perfect to hit her where she'd been standing.

He didn't like Cecile out trespassing in her search for her friend and he definitely didn't like someone shooting at her. What might have happened if he hadn't been there? Or if she hadn't bent down at just the right moment? When he thought about how close that first bullet had come to hitting its mark, he shuddered.

He'd given her leeway on her search and

managed to stall Henderson for months, but after today, he was putting a stop to Cecile's futile search efforts. He knew she wanted to find her friend, but risking her own life wasn't the way to accomplish it. He couldn't lose her, not like that.

His radio clipped to his belt came alive. "Sheriff, we need you over here on the other side of the ridge."

He glanced at Cecile. Had the others found something? He radioed back that they were on their way. Several feet behind the ridge was an open space. Flags had been inserted into the ground as markers of a large, rounded shape indicating someone was about to start digging up the ground in order to build something, possibly a pond. He spotted Zeke and several of his tech team standing over a smaller, rectangular hole in the ground within the circle of the flags. "What is it?"

Cecile glanced at the hole. A shovel lay on the ground beside it. Her green eyes locked onto his. "It's a grave, Josh, and it looks like someone recently dug it up."

His breath caught at the implication. He knelt down and examined it. Fresh dirt had been piled up—whoever had dug this hadn't bothered to shove the dirt back inside. The grave was at least five feet, deep enough to mask the scent of whatever had been buried within so animals wouldn't ravage it.

He glanced up at his forensic tech. "Is there any way to tell what was inside this?"

"Maybe. I can take soil samples. They might tell me if any match soil samples from the tarp we found buried with our Jane Doe." He glanced at each one of them. "That is what we're all thinking, right? That this was where she was buried before she was moved to the location where we found her?"

Josh looked at Cecile, then nodded. They were all on the same page. "Take your samples. And I want this area searched and photographed. Nothing gets left out."

He pulled Cecile aside. "Looks like Henderson is about to build something on this site. That would explain why the killer would move the body. What doesn't make sense is why he wouldn't close in the grave."

"Maybe he got interrupted before he could? You think Henderson is involved?"

Josh thought it over, then shook his head. "No. He wouldn't call me out here if he was."

Cecile nodded to show that she agreed. "Well, if our Jane Doe was buried here originally, the killer definitely changed his methods between when he first buried her and when he hid her a second time. This hole was deep— much deeper than the one he dug when he moved the body. According to the case files I've been looking at from the neighboring counties, I'm surprised he reburied her at all. Based on the timeline, his pattern over the past few years seems to have gone from burying his victims to dumping them on the side of the road. He's less worried about getting caught now. His confidence has grown with each kill."

"It would have to have grown for him to target you."

"There's something else, Josh. For someone to dig up and move this body, they would need to have access. A relative or employee perhaps? If, as you say, Henderson installed the motion sensors on his gates, he would know if someone was trespassing."

"That's a good point. I'm not sure when the motion sensors were installed, but I'll find out." He enjoyed bouncing ideas off Cecile, but they weren't going to find the answers standing around speculating. "You finish overseeing this. I'm going to have a talk with Henderson's security team. It's their job to know what's going on, so let's see if they do."

THREE

Josh borrowed Zeke's pickup and drove to the main gate of the ranch. The guard let him through and Frank Henderson met him in the driveway.

"Sheriff, I heard there was a commotion going on by the east gate. What's happening?"

Josh got out of his vehicle and pulled out his notebook. "My deputy and I were shot at over by the caves. When I brought a team out there to investigate the shooting, we found an empty grave."

He looked surprised. "An empty grave? Are you sure? Maybe it was just a hole in the ground that an animal dug up."

"No, this was a deliberate act, done by human hands. There was a shovel right next to it. Any idea who dug it?"

"I have no idea. No one is supposed to be

out there. I have been telling you that every time we speak. We have plans to build a pond, but that work hasn't started yet except for mapping the area. That land is supposed to be off limits."

"Well, someone shot at us. I want to know who it was and why. I'll need to speak with your head of security."

Henderson nodded. "Fine, but I want to be kept up-to-date on the investigation. If something is happening on my property, I expect to know about it."

After giving all the necessary assurances, Josh headed for the building off to the side of the main house that housed Henderson's security detail. Josh didn't understand why one rancher needed a squad of highly trained guards working for him but Henderson had the means to fund it and enough land to keep them all patrolling it. He was one of the largest landowners in the county and, from what Josh had heard, was steadily buying up any property that became available.

Josh was glad to know the Silver Star, his family's ranch, wasn't in any danger. Henderson was a vulture. His ranch was large in terms of acreage, but he didn't utilize it. He horded this precious commodity in order to build his wealth.

Josh knocked on the door, which was opened by a large man wearing a shirt that had the name Kennedy embroidered on it. The man's mannerisms screamed former military. Josh introduced himself and showed his badge. Kennedy shook his hand, then led Josh inside to his office. On the way, Josh spotted a large locker of weapons standing open in the back of the room. That was a lot of firepower. Josh couldn't help wondering why they needed it all.

"What can I do for you, Sheriff?" Kennedy asked as he settled himself into his chair.

"One of my deputies and I were on the back ridge by the caves earlier today when someone started shooting at us. Is it possible that was one of your men?"

He didn't seem fazed. "No, that couldn't have been one of us. All of my men were present for your brother's presentation this morning on tactical analysis. It was quite informative."

His brother Paul had started a business training law enforcement agencies throughout the state in tactical techniques. He'd mentioned to Josh that he was doing a training session with Henderson's security team. "Everyone was there? No one was missing?"

"I had someone guarding the main gate, of course, and a few men cleaning up an accident, but otherwise, yes, everyone was here. We broke off afterward into groups to patrol but everyone was present and accounted for until after three p.m."

"How often is that area patrolled by your team?"

"Every day. We have a team of two men who patrol that section."

"Is it the same men every time?"

"No. We rotate shifts so no one gets too used to seeing the same property. It's good to have fresh eyes."

He couldn't agree more although there was also something to be said for knowing the layout of the land. "Have any of your teams reported seeing a grave being dug behind the ridge near the caves? It's about five feet deep and freshly dug up."

Kennedy looked surprised, but only for a moment. "I don't have any reports of that. Maybe someone was trying to bury an animal. It happens. A coyote gets on the property, someone shoots it and then we have to dispose of the body."

"No one buries a coyote in a five-foot grave. That depth takes time and energy. Plus, the grave was empty. Whatever had been buried there was taken *out*, not put in."

The main door opened and both Josh and Kennedy turned to see a group of men enter the building. Kennedy stood and called to one of them. "Tom, did you fellas finish clearing up that mess?"

A man entered the doorway. Josh noticed a bruise on his left cheek, along with several other cuts and bruises on the man's arms. The two men standing behind him sported similar injuries.

Tom gave him a nod. "I had the Gator towed to the repair shed, then returned to help these two clean up the debris."

"Okay, good." Kennedy looked at Josh. "Two of our off-road vehicles overturned this morning, injuring several of my team." He turned back to Tom. "Once you three are cleaned up, I want you to head out to the east ridge and make certain it's secure."

Josh stood. "No, don't. I've got a forensics team taking samples and photographing that area now. I'd prefer if no one went near it until we've cleared it. They'll mark it with crime scene tape."

"And how long will that take, Sheriff?" He heard the annoyance in Kennedy's tone and chose to ignore it. He wasn't looking to antagonize anyone, but he wasn't going to back down from doing his job, either.

"Depends on what we find."

Tom stepped fully into the room and glanced from Kennedy to Josh. "And what are you expecting to find?"

"We recovered a Jane Doe yesterday, in a shallow grave in the woods. She'd been surprisingly well preserved, leading us to speculate that she'd been buried deep for a long period before she was dug up and moved. At five feet—the depth of the grave we found on this property—the body would have remained intact."

"Are you saying you believe someone buried a body on this property, then dug it up and moved it elsewhere?"

"That's exactly what I'm saying."

Kennedy's jaw clenched. "Not on my watch." He glanced at Tom, who shook his head.

"I haven't seen anything like that and no one has mentioned it, either."

Josh just shrugged. "Well, there's a big hole in the ground. You're welcome to go look at it. Just don't touch it and don't go too near it until the forensics come back clean." He held out his phone and showed Kennedy a photo of the grave.

The man's face went grim and his neck muscles tightened. "Have you spoken with Mr. Henderson about this?"

"I just had a conversation with him. He understands our presence here isn't negotiable, at least not until we finish this investigation. Then, of course, there's the matter of the person who shot at my deputy and me."

"I don't know anything about that."

"Mr. Kennedy, you just told me nothing happens on your watch. So either one of your men shot at us, or you've dropped the ball on monitoring people on your boss's property."

Kennedy motioned for Tom and the others to leave. They walked off as Kennedy shut the door and turned back to face Josh. "I'll tell my guys not to disturb the site but I can't promise there won't be trespassers who do. It's a big issue for us."

Josh was sure he was referring to Cecile and her search, but he wouldn't apologize for her, not to this guy. Her search had yielded something after all, something that might be a crucial clue to solving this serial case.

"I understand motion sensors were installed on the gates to deal with trespassers. When were those put in place?"

"We started placing the sensors two days ago, but we haven't finished yet. Some gates still don't have them."

So whoever had dug up that body could have done it without being noticed even if they were trespassing. "Thanks for your help. I'll be in touch if I need anything else."

Josh noticed Tom and the others watching him as he left the building and walked to his pickup, mulling over what to make of all of this. He didn't care for Henderson but he didn't peg the man as a killer. Still, he couldn't rule him out.

But why shoot at them?

That part didn't make sense.

He slipped off his cowboy hat and placed it on the seat beside him, then checked in with his team. He drove off the Henderson Ranch and onto the main roadway.

Something was going on in his town and he was determined to find out what it was.

The medical examiner sounded irritated when Cecile questioned her again about an identification on their Jane Doe. She'd had the body for days and they were no closer to identifying her than when they'd found her.

Someone was missing their daughter.

"I've reached out to dentists in the area to try to find a match on dental records but so far there haven't been any. I'm continuing the work on it, Deputy."

"What about DNA?"

"We were able to extract DNA from the bone marrow but it'll be weeks before we get those results back. Even then, she'd have to have her DNA on file somewhere in order for us to make a match."

Cecile hung up the phone, irritated by the slow process. The forensics collected at the scene hadn't offered much in the way of evidence, either, but someone out there had to be missing this Jane Doe.

She pulled up a list of missing-persons reports in the county, then filtered it by gender. Erica's name popped out at her and her gut clenched. Could their murdered Jane Doe be Erica? If she'd originally been in the empty grave they'd found on Henderson's land as they suspected, it was possible. But Cecile wasn't getting her hopes up. The oldest victim they'd connected to this serial so far had been killed five years earlier. Erica had been missing for ten. And the necklace she'd discovered by the caves proved that other women had been on the property. If she couldn't find Erica, she could at least give another woman's family closure by identifying this victim.

Cecile glanced at the silver necklace still housed in the plastic evidence bag on her desk. It was nondescript, with no engraving and no way to determine whom it belonged to. She didn't recall her friend ever owning such a necklace, plus she doubted it would still be this shiny ten years later even if she had. She'd run it for prints but they'd found none that could be lifted. Whatever evidence it had once contained was gone, probably lost to the elements.

She'd considered putting a plea out on social media for anyone who knew the owner of it but she wasn't certain that was the smart move. Not yet. It probably belonged to someone who'd been out there exploring the caves and had no connection to their Jane Doe or the murderer, but she wasn't jumping to any conclusions.

She put the necklace away and tried to concentrate on her cases. She assigned two of the task force members—Lansing from Leake County and Miller from Mead County—the

job of going through the missing persons list
and seeing if any of them had been resolved.
Runaways often came home. Women who'd
fled abusive relationships often returned to
them. In those cases, the police were rarely
notified that the person missing had been
found so the case could be closed. She needed
to have an accurate account of women in the
area who were still missing. It might help narrow down who their Jane Doe was.

She still had loads of cases from different
counties to dig through. She spent the next
several hours reading up about the personal
lives of the victims and examining the physical and forensic evidence of women who had
been brutally murdered, and she shuddered
at each one.

Being an investigator meant she saw the
worst of the worst, but this level of brutality
shook her. How could people be so evil? And
how could they walk around looking like everyone else while committing such acts?

Logically, evil should look evil but she
knew that wasn't true. She knew it from years
of investigative work but also from years of
Sunday school. Even the enemy disguised
himself as something good. That was exactly
what men like this killer did. He disguised

himself every day in public, showing his true nature only to his unfortunate victims.

She pushed away the latest case file, placing it into the stack of confirmed cases tied to the serial killer. The physical evidence of strangulation, stab wounds and traces of gas and oil on the bodies, the signature knot, all pointed to the connection. That made eleven victims over nine years—and those were only the ones they knew about. There could easily be others, buried deep and undiscovered. This guy had been active. He'd also been smart. According to the timeline they were forming, he moved between jurisdictions between each kill, probably in an effort to conceal the extent of his activity from each sheriff's department.

She wanted to take a break, but she'd already spent a lot of time out at the scene on the Henderson Ranch. She needed to sit here and go through these cases.

She forced herself to pick up another case file. She opened it and read about the victim. Nineteen-year-old Madison Winslow. Found murdered in Butler County two years earlier after going missing from a bonfire party hosted by a schoolmate. There had been the usual drinking and recreational drug use although Madison's friends had insisted there had been no heavy usage. No one had seen who she'd gone off with, either.

She sighed as the memory of the night Erica had vanished came rushing back to her. This girl's disappearance mirrored Erica's in every way except that her body had been found while Erica's was still missing. Cecile pulled out the photograph of the pretty blonde in her graduation gown smiling big for the camera. Her whole life must have been in front of her when this picture had been taken. Just like Erica, she would've had plans and expectations of what her future would be like. And, also like Erica's, her plans had been ended by a maniac.

Cecile glanced at the necklace around the girl's neck in the photograph. She stiffened and sat up straight. The silver chain around the victim's neck looked familiar...too familiar.

She grabbed the evidence bag and held it up to the photograph of Madison Winslow. It was a match.

She'd just found whom this necklace belonged to. Its owner had been murdered two years earlier by the serial killer they were hunting.

What then was her necklace doing at the caves on the Henderson Ranch?

"The empty grave. Now, this necklace. That area has to be some sort of dumping ground for the killer, Josh." Cecile was fired up and talking a mile a minute.

He leaned back in his chair and listened to what she had to say. It did seem odd that the necklace belonging to one of their victims had been found on the ranch, but it wasn't enough to get a warrant. "Madison Winslow wasn't found there. Her body was dumped in Butler County, at least forty miles from the Henderson Ranch. We can't compel another search of the property because of that. Henderson will just say the victim must have trespassed on his property at some point and we can't refute that. We have to wait for the lab results to come back in on the gravesite before we can expand our search."

Cecile huffed in frustration. "Even if the grave does turn out to belong to our Jane Doe, we still can't prove the killer didn't trespass to bury her there and to exhume her."

"I know, but at least it's something." He fingered the necklace. "It does look like the one in the photograph but we first need to make certain it belonged to her—and that she had it with her on the night she was killed. For all we know, she could have lost it prior to that night."

Cecile settled her hands on her hips and bit her lip. He could actually see her mind working trying to put the puzzle pieces together. If anyone could, it was her. "I'll drive over to her parents' house and ask them."

"Good idea. I'll come with you." He stood and pulled on his jacket.

Instead of being pleased, she seemed put out. "I don't need a babysitter, Josh."

"I don't think you do. I just want to go. Okay?"

She shrugged her agreement, then walked to grab her gun and keys.

He couldn't explain why he wanted to go except that the idea of the two of them in a car together struck him as nice. He liked her and enjoyed her company. If things were different, he could see a future with her. But things *weren't* different.

Why was he setting them both up for failure?

Cecile was the one person, aside from his family, he was certain didn't believe he'd had a hand in Haley's murder. He'd given her the file, even asked her opinion on the case years ago and she'd uncovered some solid leads for him to explore. Unfortunately, they hadn't gone anywhere and Haley's killer was still on the loose.

He let her drive and climbed into the passenger seat of her pickup. She was on the highway before she looked at him. "What's this really about, Josh? You've never left the office to go interview a possible witness."

She knew him so well. It was what made them work so well together. He had a sudden, unsettling thought about how much harder his job would be if he didn't have her by his side. He knew the question would startle her, coming out of the blue, but he couldn't help asking, "You're not going to take that job, are you, Cecile?"

She gripped the steering wheel tighter and sighed. He'd expected—hoped for—an instant denial. Her hesitation made his gut clench.

"I don't know what I'm going to do, Josh. Like I told you, I turned down the job offer. And I do have plenty of reasons to stay. My family, my work, Erica… On the other hand, I also know I'm ready for a change in my life. Maybe I've been in a holding pattern for far too long. Maybe it's time for something else."

"I don't want to lose you, Cecile." He reached across the seat and touched her hand.

She glanced at it, then back at the road. "You don't want to lose me as an investigator?"

"No, I don't. I absolutely don't. I'll do anything you want. Tell me what I can do to keep you here."

Her face reddened and she shifted uncomfortably in her seat. Suddenly he knew exactly what it would take to get her to stay. His commitment to more than a job.

He swallowed hard. This wasn't the direction he'd hoped this conversation would take. "Cecile, you know—"

"Don't," she told him, holding up her hand. "Don't you dare give me a bunch of excuses." She pulled up to a house and threw the truck into gear before turning to him. "Either you want me or you don't, Josh. It's that simple."

She got out of the truck and the force of the slam of the door told him the true extent of her anger. She'd placed the ball strictly in his court. He could make her stay with three little words.

Unfortunately for them both, they were words he'd sworn to never say to another woman again.

* * *

Cecile got out of the truck and walked to the front door of the house. Josh followed her. She wanted to tell him to let her do the talking, but if she spoke to him in that moment, she might start yelling. She took a deep breath and forced herself to focus. She needed to cool down if she was going to face these already grieving parents with this new information.

She rang the doorbell. A woman answered the door and flashed a bright smile before she saw their badges, then her face dropped. Probably reliving the day the Butler County Sheriff's Office had given her the news about her daughter.

"Yes? What can I help you with?"

"May we come inside and speak with you, Mrs. Winslow?"

She opened the door wider and allowed them inside. When they reached the living room, a man appeared. He slipped off his reading glasses and glanced at his wife. "What's this?"

"We would like to ask you both a few questions," Cecile told them. "I'm Deputy Cecile Richardson. This is Sheriff Avery from Courtland County."

"What does the Courtland County Sheriff's Office want with us?" Mr. Winslow asked.

Cecile pulled the plastic bag from her pocket and held it out. "We were hoping you could tell us if this belonged to your daughter."

Mrs. Winslow took the bag and fingered the necklace. Her expression turned to grief. "It's Madison's."

"Are you certain?"

"Definitely. It's hers. We never knew what happened to it. We had to bury her without it."

"Do you remember if she was wearing it the day she was killed?"

Mr. Winslow scowled. "She always wore it. Never took it off."

"Is it possible she lost it sometime in the days before she was killed?"

Mrs. Winslow shook her head, looking like she was on the verge of tears. "No, she was wearing it the last time I saw her that morning when she left the house. When the police couldn't find it, we searched the house looking for it. Where did you find it?"

"Near a cave in Courtland. Do you know if she ever went to the Henderson Ranch?"

Mrs. Winslow looked to her husband, but

he shook his head before saying, "I never heard her mention it. I don't know why she would. That's quite a way off."

"Is it possible there was a party near there?"

"I really don't know," Mrs. Winslow admitted. "You'd have to ask her friends. The local police said she'd gone to a party but it was in Butler County, not Courtland."

Cecile sighed. Another dead end. She held out her hand to retrieve the necklace. Mrs. Winslow seemed hesitant to return it.

"Will I get it back? It's just…we have so little left of Madison."

"Right now, it's possibly evidence," Josh told her, his voice soft and understanding. "We have to keep it, but once the case is closed, I'll make certain you get it back."

"Thank you," she said but her husband wasn't so generous.

"You mean *if* the case gets closed. It's been two years and none of y'all are any closer to finding my daughter's killer than the day she was found."

Cecile understood his frustration. "We've partnered with several other law enforcement agencies in the area including Butler County to form a task force. It'll help us to work more in conjunction and share information that should make it easier to find whoever did this."

Mrs. Winslow gasped. "I saw this on the news. Are you saying our daughter was killed by a…by a…serial killer?"

"It is possible," Cecile agreed. "As I said, we're going through cases from several different counties to try to determine which ones fit the pattern."

Mrs. Winslow put her hands over her face and sobbed. "It's not right. Madison was such a good girl. Everyone loved her. She had such a bright future ahead of her."

Her husband hugged her tightly, then turned to them. "Find this monster. Please. Our daughter deserves justice."

Cecile nodded and assured them they would do their best. She'd tried to brace for an emotional scene, but dealing with grieving families was never something you could really prepare for. She felt their pain and empathized, thanks to the loss she'd experienced. She hadn't been a member of Erica's family, yet she'd grieved her disappearance just the same.

They saw themselves out and it wasn't until the chill in the air hit her that Cecile realized a tear had slipped onto her cheek. She quickly brushed it away. Josh didn't need to see her whimpering, too. Besides, she had a job to do and her breaking down wasn't going to do anyone any good.

They walked to the truck. Josh shook his head and stuffed his hands into his pockets. "That was brutal."

"Yes, it was. They're still grieving their daughter. Every day that her murderer walks free is a day they're denied justice."

"I don't think learning their daughter was possibly killed by a serial killer helped anything."

She shook her head. "No, it didn't." She empathized with this grieving family. The idea of learning that Erica had been murdered by a serial killer would be horrific. Murder was terrible at any time but knowing that the last face your loved one saw was that of a monster was beyond terrifying.

She shuddered at the idea.

"You okay?" Josh asked her.

She gave him a curt nod of her head as they climbed into her truck and she got the engine running. He didn't need to know how having this maniac targeting women in her town bothered her. She didn't want to appear weak in front of him.

"I'm fine. I'm just cold. It's turned chilly since the sun set." It wasn't all a lie but it wasn't the complete truth, either. She reached over and clicked on the heater to break the chill in the air, then pulled onto the road to head back to the sheriff's office.

Josh raised a brow and closed the vents on his side before aiming the center one at her. "Well, I'm burning up with anger that someone like that is operating in my county and we don't have any good leads yet."

"The investigation is just starting. We don't even have the forensic results back yet on our Jane Doe. Plus, we've only been through a handful of the case files from the other jurisdictions." She checked the vent but didn't feel any warm air flowing out yet, so she inched the heater up another notch.

"I know. I'm just impatient. Now that we're taking the lead on this, it's going to reflect on our office if we drop the ball. I want to make certain everything is by the book and proper. I don't want any wrong moves."

"I know how to conduct an investigation, Josh." Annoyance bit into her tone.

"I know you do, Cecile."

"Then why say that? In fact, why comment on this at all? I am the lead investigator, aren't

I? I am the one Sheriff Milton wanted, wasn't I?" Another chill rushed through her. She put her hand over the vent. The air still wasn't hot. It wasn't even warm. She pounded her hand against the vent. "Why isn't this heater working?"

"Calm down," Josh said, which kicked her aggravation up another gear. She hated feeling like she was being patronized or placated. "Of course, you're the lead investigator and, yes, you know what you're doing, but you're not the only one with a stake in this, Cecile."

She felt a little woozy. Somewhere inside, an internal alarm bell went off, telling her that something was wrong, but she ignored it, focusing on the argument at hand. "I'm sick to death of you taking me for granted, Josh. You know I've had other offers. Offers for more money and bigger departments. You might not want me, but other people do."

"I do want you, Cecile."

Suddenly, she lost her composure. She'd had enough of his hesitancy. "But as what, Josh? Some genderless best buddy who you never would think to give a second look? I'm a great catch, Josh Avery. Not that you ever bothered to notice."

Those internal alarm bells were ringing

louder now, telling her that this wasn't like her. She always kept it together—she never dumped her heart out on the floor for everyone to see. Unease grew in the pit of her stomach. What was wrong with her? What was muddling her head and unraveling her control until all of this came spilling out?

"What?" Josh sounded completely baffled. "When did this become about you and me?"

"It always has been about us, Josh." The words poured from her without a filter and she grew increasingly panicky when she realized she wasn't able to hold them back. "Don't you see that everything is about us? You're the reason I'm still in Courtland. You're the only reason I'm still here. If you don't want me, why should I stick around?"

"Cecile—"

"No!" She rubbed her hand against her eyes. Her eyelids were heavy and she was suddenly very sleepy. Everything slowed to a crawl and she had trouble focusing on the road in front of her.

"Cecile, what's going on? What's wrong with you?"

"I—I don't…" *I don't know,* she wanted to scream. *I don't know, but something is definitely, dangerously wrong.*

Her tongue felt thick and heavy and weirdly disconnected from her thoughts, but a few more words managed to slip out. "I'm not enough for you." Tears sprang in her eyes and she couldn't stop them. "We could be so great, but you won't take the risk because I'm not enough."

The truck swerved and Josh reached for the wheel. "Cecile, something's wrong. Pull over, pull over now!"

She tried to obey, but she couldn't get her body to cooperate. Her head felt like it was full of cotton and her eyes could no longer focus on the road.

But before she could tell him so, everything went dark.

Cecile slumped over the steering wheel. Josh grabbed for it but the truck veered into another lane and he wasn't fast enough to stop it. To his relief, there weren't any cars close enough to risk a collision—but their situation was far from safe. The truck was out of his control, he was panicking over Cecile's condition…and he could feel his own head fogging up, no doubt because of whatever had affected her.

They needed to pull over so he could check on Cecile and call for help. He tried to get to the emergency brake but it was by Cecile's foot. No way he was reaching that. As he struggled to think, he kept one hand on the wheel and used the other to roll down the window and suck in some fresh air. It helped clear his head. He knew what he had to do. He had to reach the gear shift or shut off the engine and pull the truck over, but both were on the other side of the truck. He unbuckled his seat belt and tried scooting over to stop them.

He wasn't fast enough. The truck veered off the road, tossing him backward against the door as it rammed its way through the brush before finally splashing into a pond.

He shut off the engine. He couldn't say for sure what they'd been breathing in—perhaps exhaust, since that would explain the confusion and disorientation—but whatever it was, they were definitely better off without it. Next priority was to get them out of the truck before it sank.

He unclipped the seat belt of an unconscious Cecile, then kicked open her door and climbed out, gasping as the cold water stabbed him. Despite the discomfort, he was grateful for the way it helped clear his head. Of course, with clarity came an increased awareness of their precarious situation.

He reached for Cecile and pulled her into the water. She roused momentarily in his arms as the cold water hit her.

"What—what happened?" Her voice was groggy and she wasn't completely awake, but she flung her arms around his shoulders and rested her head against him as she drifted off again.

She needed medical attention. Josh did his best to keep her head above water as he swam toward the bank. When he could stand, he lifted her from the water and carried her, setting her down on the grass. She was shivering and so was he. When he pulled his cell phone out of his pocket, he found it too waterlogged to even turn on. He would have to hike up the embankment to the road and try to flag down a car for help.

He turned and watched Cecile's truck sink into the murky water. She wouldn't be happy when she awoke but at least she was alive.

He breathed in the fresh air and his head cleared even more. He could only hope the fresh air was helping Cecile as well, but since she was unconscious, he couldn't be sure. He knelt beside her and pressed his fingers against her wrist. Her pulse was slow but she was still alive and breathing.

Relief flooded him along with a sudden urge to take her into his arms and hold her. She was shivering but he couldn't even offer her his coat since it was dripping wet, too. He touched her face, remembering her words to him and wondering how she could ever believe she wasn't enough. She was incredible in every way. What more could there possibly be?

But they could debate that later. His top priority had to be getting them help. "I'll be back," he whispered before hurrying up the hill to the main road.

He saw headlights coming toward him, so he stepped out into the road and waved his hands. When the car slowed, he hurried to the driver's window. "There's been an accident. We need an ambulance. Can I use your phone?"

The driver agreed and offered his cell phone. Josh placed a call to dispatch, then ran back down to wait with Cecile until help arrived. He didn't like leaving her alone for even a few minutes. The motorist who had loaned him the phone remained at the top of the hill and flagged down the deputies when they arrived.

"She needs help," Josh called once he saw them coming.

Zeke hurried to him while Greg grabbed the first aid kit. "Ambulance is on the way."

"What happened to her?" Zeke asked him.

"There was something wrong with the vents. They started pumping out something that messed with our heads. I'd closed my vent, but hers were wide open, so she got the brunt of it. Plus, she's a lot smaller than me, so it hit her harder. She started driving erratically, and then she lost consciousness. Next thing I know, we're veering off the road and into the lake."

"You should get looked at, too," Greg told him.

"Once the ambulance arrives and gets her settled, I want you to oversee pulling her vehicle out of the water. Something happened in that truck. I want to know what it was."

"Will do, Sheriff."

The ambulance arrived and Josh watched them treat Cecile. Someone handed him a towel and he did his best to dry off but he wasn't worried about himself. Every thought was about Cecile and trying to wrap his brain around what had happened.

He couldn't seem to shake off the helplessness he'd felt at watching her. Unable to do anything to help her. He hadn't even realized something was wrong—that they were under attack—until it was almost too late.

How and why had this happened? Those were the two questions he needed answers to. Whoever had done this had obviously hoped to incapacitate her and maybe even kill her.

He walked back up to the street. Everything looked normal except for the hole in the overgrowth where the truck had gone down the embankment.

He approached Greg. "I'm going to the hospital. I want someone going over that truck ASAP and I want to know the moment they figure out what happened."

Whatever this assailant was after, he wasn't going to get it. Josh wasn't going to allow this maniac to get to her again. He wasn't letting another person he cared about be harmed.

FOUR

Someone was holding her head underwater. At least, that was how it felt as Cecile awoke. She'd had surgery once on her shoulder after falling off a horse, so she recognized the lingering feeling of anesthesia. But what had she had surgery for?

She forced her eyes to open and spotted a monitor beeping beside her and an IV in her arm, confirming she was in a hospital. Her mind fought to remember how she'd gotten here. The last thing she recalled was being in the truck with Josh after interviewing Madison Winslow's parents.

And she…she'd been driving and arguing with Josh. She'd felt woozy and said things she couldn't believe had come out of her mouth. Embarrassment filled her for only a moment before worry reared its head. Had they been in an accident? Had Josh been hurt?

She stiffened and tried to push back the blankets that covered her. She had to find Josh.

She stopped when she spotted him stretched out in the chair by the bed. He was dressed in hospital scrubs and was slouched over, his head bowed and his hands pressed together. As the fuzziness from her head cleared, she realized he was praying. Whispered prayers on her behalf.

She watched him for half a minute, enthralled by such an intimate moment, before her movement grabbed his attention and he sat up straight.

His face broke into a relieved smile. "You're awake. How are you feeling?" He reached for her hand and clutched it.

"A little groggy. What happened? I feel like I'm coming off anesthesia. Did I have to have surgery?"

"No. You passed out while driving and the truck ended up in the lake. You've been in and out of it for several hours now. But no surgery."

She had no memory of driving into the lake but a quick image flashed through her mind—her pressing against him as he carried her from the water. Warmth filled her face but she didn't dare comment on that moment.

He'd simply been saving her from drowning. On to practical matters. "My truck?"

"The water damage is extensive. I've got Joe Thomas looking at it to try to find out what happened. I think something went wrong with the vents, resulting in us breathing in exhaust or something else."

That might account for the residual grogginess she was experiencing.

"What do you remember?" he asked.

"Not much." It was all a jumbled mess inside her brain. "I remember trying to make the heater work. It was cold but no heat was coming out—which makes sense, if there was a problem with the vents."

His hand was still holding hers and she didn't try to pull away. She liked the comforting feeling.

"I called your father. He said he'd be by in the morning to check on you."

He didn't drive, so morning was probably the earliest he could get someone to give him a ride.

"Josh, I haven't noticed anything out of the ordinary with my truck recently. Do you think this was intentional—that someone tampered with the vents?" The memories of the shooting at Henderson Ranch and the attack on her home were still fresh in her mind.

"Let's wait and see before we start jumping to conclusions. Joe is still examining the truck. Plus, the doctors are still running tests to figure out what happened to you. Did you take anything? Feel any pain before you blacked out? Or maybe you ate or drank something that could have been spiked?"

"I didn't have anything in the truck. The last thing I ate or drank before going to the Winslows' was at the sheriff's office—and I don't think it would have taken that long to kick in." She'd felt fine during the whole forty-minute drive to the Winslows'. "I don't think I was poisoned. Could this have been something natural? A medical condition maybe?" She'd felt fine earlier but knew some conditions could come on suddenly.

He rubbed his chin, something he did when he was thinking. "It's possible. The doctors are giving you a full workup. If it was something medical, they'll figure it out. But I've got to say… I don't think that's likely. Whatever happened affected me, too, so it's not like it was just you. In the meantime, I've got our guys checking out the truck and canvassing the area. Maybe someone saw something."

She hoped so. But now that he'd brought up that he'd been affected, too, she was worried about him. "How are you? How badly did it affect you?"

"I'm okay. I felt a little off but it cleared up. I shut off my vents, remember? And given the difference in our sizes, even if we'd gotten the same dose, it probably would have hit you harder."

"So if this was an attack," she said, trying to force her fuzzy mind to think it through, "what was the attacker after? Did he want me to die in the crash? That's not his usual method. Our killer likes things just so—but with an attack like this, there's too much left to chance. There's no way anyone could have known we would end up in the lake."

"I've wondered about that myself. The only answer I can come up with is that he thought you'd survive the crash but be knocked out or injured, and it would be his chance to abduct you. The last time he tried to grab you, you fought him off. Maybe he was trying to get you alone and incapacitated so he'd finally be able to grab you this time."

"Why would he do that knowing you were in the truck with me?"

"He probably thought you'd be alone. Don't forget, I decided at the last minute to go with you. Maybe it caught him by surprise, too, but it was too late to do anything. He must have messed with the vents before we left—but we didn't notice on the drive because you didn't try to turn on the heat. Once you did, on the drive back, you kept saying the heater wasn't working correctly, remember?"

She had a vague memory of that and it did explain how she was feeling now. Suddenly another memory tugged at her. A memory of her calling Josh out. "What else did I say?"

This time, his face reddened and he rubbed the back of his neck. "You don't remember?"

"Not really, no." It had to be bad based on the antsy way he was reacting. "What was it? Something embarrassing?"

"No, you have nothing to be embarrassed about, Cecile."

His phone dinged. He pulled it from his pocket and glanced at the screen. Cecile noticed that it was different from his usual phone. He saw her staring and answered her unspoken question. "My phone got waterlogged when we went into the lake. This is a pay-as-you-go that I picked up from the shop across the street. Anyway, the message is from Colby. He brought me a change of clothes and is offering me a ride back to the sheriff's office. I'll call and check on you later." He leaned down and planted a kiss on her forehead. The machine that monitored her pulse sped up beeping. Josh acted oblivious to the machine's reaction as he picked up a plastic bag with his clothes and a separate bag that seemed to be full of rice and probably held his soaked phone. He walked out while Cecile wanted to crawl beneath the covers to hide her humiliation.

She leaned back against her pillows and tried to steady her pulse, silently fuming at the machine for giving away her feelings. There was no way he'd missed her reaction to his kiss. He knew her feeling for him, yet he continued pushing her away.

Just further proof that no matter what she did, he was never going to return her feelings.

Colby waited for Josh by the elevator. He handed him a bag with a change of clothes and another pair of boots. Josh ducked into the restroom to change, then returned the scrubs he'd borrowed from the nurse.

Colby held the elevator doors open as he

waited for Josh. His brother had a knowing look on his face. "What?" Josh asked but Colby only shook his head.

Josh could have gotten a ride from one of the deputies, but knowing his brother was in town for the anniversary party, he'd first called Colby. They'd grown closer over the past few months after Colby had taken a break from the FBI and come to stay with him. Colby had been going through a tough time after his girlfriend had been murdered, and he'd needed support from someone who "got it." Josh was glad he could fill that need for his brother, though the common tie that bound them together was something that he prayed the remainder of their siblings would never experience—the senseless, violent death of someone they each cared about. In Colby's case, it had been his physician girlfriend who'd been murdered after discovering fraudulent claims were being submitted using her name and provider identification number. For Josh, it had been Haley's murder.

Thankfully, Colby had been able to solve Tessa's murder and find love again with her cousin Brooke, but Josh had yet to move on. He couldn't. Not when Haley's murder remained unsolved.

As they walked to Colby's SUV, the smirk on his brother's face remained. "Spit it out, Colby," Josh told him.

His brother stopped walking and looked at him. "I was just wondering what was going on with you and Cecile."

That was unexpected. "I don't know what you mean."

"After I sent you that text, I came upstairs. I wanted to see how she was doing. I saw you holding her hand and, I've gotta say, Josh, it looked intimate."

Josh nearly choked on the next breath he took. He quickly cleared his throat. His face warmed but he did his best to pass it off as nothing. "I don't know what you think you saw but we were in an accident. I was just making sure she was okay. That's all." He fumbled over the word "accident." He wasn't calling it an attack yet, not until he had all the facts, but he was sure in his gut that this had been an intentional act against her.

"You've both been acting weird around each other ever since I got back to town. Even Brooke noticed it."

He inwardly groaned. He'd known his feelings for Cecile had changed but he hadn't realized it was that obvious to other people.

But, he reminded himself, his brother wasn't just people. "It's obvious?"

"Look, I wouldn't normally bring it up. Your personal life is your own business. And for what it's worth, I've always thought you and Cecile were good together."

They reached Colby's SUV and Josh climbed inside. He sighed. His brother was right. They had always been good together until…

He removed his hat and ran a hand through his hair. "Things have been a little tense between us for a few weeks now."

"Did something happen?"

Oh boy, had something happened. "I kissed her."

Colby's eyes widened and he leaned back in his seat.

"I don't even know how it happened," Josh admitted. "It just did. Now everything between us has changed." His face warmed at the memory, mostly out of shame because he knew he could never have her, but also because of how good that kiss had felt. The memory of her in his arms still lingered.

"So then what's the problem? Why do you look like someone just kicked your cat?"

"Because it shouldn't have happened. It

can't go anywhere, Colby. I'm still a suspect in Haley's murder. I can't get involved with someone with that hanging over my head."

"Surely Cecile doesn't believe you had anything to do with that?"

"No, she doesn't, but plenty of other people do. I can't ask her or anyone to live under a cloud like that."

"What cloud? There's no cloud of suspicion, Josh. Sure, there are a few people who might throw that accusation at you—like that vulture reporter, Dirk Whatshisname—but everyone who truly knows you believes in you. That's why they elected you. You can't let a few small-minded people hold you back from falling in love again." A grin spread across Colby's face. "Trust me. Let it happen. You'll be ecstatic."

His brother was newly engaged and still enjoying the headiness of the happiness he'd found with Brooke. But he'd never been suspected of murder. He'd never lived with that stain on his reputation.

"I can't ask Cecile—or anyone—to shoulder that. It wouldn't be fair to her."

"I don't think she would mind."

"Maybe not today, but what about years from now? She'll grow to resent it. She'll grow to resent *me* when everyone starts referring to her as the killer's wife."

"Sounds to me like you're scared, Josh. Scared to take another chance on love. You and Cecile could be good together but you're too afraid of risking your heart again after what happened to Haley."

Josh sighed and pulled on his seat belt. He should have known Colby wouldn't understand his concerns. No one who hadn't been through what he had could ever understand. "Let's go. I want to stop by Joe Thomas's garage. He's looking at Cecile's truck to see if he can figure out what happened."

After a moment, Colby turned in his seat, started the engine and drove him back to town. He pulled up in front of the garage and Josh hopped out. "I'll only be a minute."

He walked toward the side door where he spotted Cecile's truck up on the rack. Joe Thomas knew more about cars than any other person Josh had ever known. He was Josh's first call whenever any crime of an automotive nature occurred in the county. Josh had even sent him to some forensics classes to aid in his understanding of how he could help the sheriff's office.

Today was one of those days when his knowledge was going to pay off.

"How's it going, Joe?" he asked when he spotted his friend leaning over the engine of another car.

"Hey, Josh."

"You got some news for me?"

Joe wiped grease from his hands on a cloth, then tucked it into his pocket. "I do, but you're not going to like it."

He was already suspecting that. Cecile's truck had been towed here less than two hours ago. If Joe had already moved on to another vehicle, it must not have taken him long to uncover the issue.

"What did you find?" He held his breath and braced himself for the answer.

"Definitely sabotage." He climbed down into a service station bay and Josh followed him. "Take a look at this." He pointed toward a large canister on the table. "It didn't take me long to find this attached to the air conditioning system. Someone tapped into it and rigged it to blow out nitrous oxide instead of hot or cold air."

Shock and anger filled him but he did his best to remain calm. He was glad to see the canister had been placed into an evidence bag and labeled. "We'll need to have it checked for fingerprints. Have you called it in yet?"

"Yeah, I phoned over to the forensics office and they're coming over to get it."

Josh doubted they would find any but the assailant could have made a mistake. He also needed to check to see if nitrous oxide was regulated by the FDA or if anyone could purchase it. He examined the canister. It was unmarked, which meant it was likely easily attainable.

"Any reason why someone would do this?" Josh asked.

"Only one reason I know of—to incapacitate the driver. Nitrous oxide isn't exactly harmful. It's the stuff dentists use to help relax you when you have a procedure. But it's definitely not something you should be exposed to while you're trying to drive."

Just as Josh had predicted. This assailant had meant to incapacitate Cecile in order to get closer to her. Only, it hadn't made her relax. It had apparently lowered her inhibitions too, based on how she'd spoken to him. She wasn't usually so open with her feelings.

He thanked Joe, then walked back to Colby's truck and climbed inside.

Colby looked at him expectantly. "Well? What's the verdict?"

"Not an accident." Josh slammed the door shut and buckled up. While he'd known it wasn't likely, he'd still been hoping for some kind of mechanical malfunction. Now he knew for certain it had been an intentional attack.

Someone had targeted Cecile again—and it seemed almost certain that it was the serial killer who had already taken at least a dozen lives.

Next time, Josh might not be there to stop his plan.

The ride to the sheriff's office was quiet but Colby spoke again as Josh opened the door to exit the SUV.

"Hey, look, I'm sorry about earlier. I shouldn't have stuck my nose in where it didn't belong. I just want to see my brother as happy as I am."

Josh didn't begrudge Colby his happiness. In fact, he envied it. But his brother couldn't possibly understand his situation—and boiling it down to Josh simply being scared didn't help. "Thanks for the ride, Colby. I'll talk to you later."

"Everyone will have eaten by now, but should I tell Mom to save you some supper?" Colby and Brooke were staying at the main house on the ranch with his folks along with Miles and his family. Josh had technically been living there, too, ever since the cabin he and Haley built had been blown up by men targeting Colby and Brooke as they searched for her cousin's murderer, but he mostly slept on the couch in his office.

He shook his head. "No. Tell her I'll call her later to check in."

His mother was used to cooking for a houseful of people and he knew that she relished having the whole noisy crew around again this week with all the kids and their spouses home for the anniversary party. She certainly wouldn't miss his presence, not with grandkids around to spoil, but she would worry when she learned about this event and want to hear from him.

Josh walked to his office, still mulling over Colby's observation that he was afraid. It couldn't be true, could it? No, his reluctance didn't stem from fear but from a deep sense of responsibility. He was only thinking about Cecile and what might happen to her in the future if they tried to move forward in a relationship. It would be amazing at first but would eventually turn into a disaster as her resentment grew. As it would. But as he stared at the photo of Haley on his desk, Colby's words kept replaying in his head. Was it possible they were both right? Was his fear of again losing someone he loved part of the reason he was holding himself back? Was he pushing her away to guard his own heart?

Cecile had practically told him the same thing.

Cecile.

He was going to lose her eventually, probably to another department, and that day was coming sooner rather than later. He felt it in his bones. The only way to make her stay was to take a risk on their relationship.

But that wasn't a risk he was willing to take, not yet. Maybe not ever.

His eye caught on the whiteboard Cecile had created in the conference room. He could see it through the glass, could see the photos of the victims lined up one by one. He sucked in a breath. They had a killer on the loose and it appeared he'd set his sights on Cecile.

If Josh was going to lose her, it wouldn't be to someone like that.

It had only been a few hours since he'd left her at the hospital but she would want to know about his findings. He grabbed his keys, then hesitated. He didn't have to go see her. A simple phone call would suffice, but the pull of seeing her, of making sure she was safe, was strong.

His willpower was stronger.

He set down his keys and took off his coat. It was time he got used to the idea that he couldn't have her. And with that in mind, he couldn't keep giving in to the desire to be around her. It wasn't fair to her.

He had to back off. It was the best thing for them both.

Cecile closed her eyes and tried to relax. Her body ached, though, and her limbs still felt heavy from whatever she'd inhaled. In contrast to her sluggish body, her mind was racing with a thousand things she needed to handle. She had to find out what exactly she'd been dosed with and how they'd done it. Someone had gotten close enough to rig her truck. That was way too close.

But Josh had assured her he was handling that. He would find out how this had happened. And it was possible they already knew why. Was he right that the killer was still out there targeting her? Had this been planned to weaken her for the attack? That thought gave her some satisfaction at the implicit acknowledgment that he couldn't incapacitate her without help. Serial killers craved a sense of power over their victims, but she wasn't going to make overpowering her easy for him. She'd knocked that lesson into him via her elbow to his face. He should know better than to attack someone with training.

The door opened and she jerked up in the bed. She was still so high on alert that she couldn't rest, though some of the tension in her eased when she realized it was only a nurse entering her room. "Relax, I'm only here to change your IV." He was dressed in scrubs along with a face mask and a cap over his head. He must have noticed her confusion about the mask. "Don't worry about this. It's just a precaution. My daughter has a cold and I don't want to pass it along to any of my patients."

She relaxed again. That made sense. He fiddled with her IV bag while she did her best to try to rest.

But that voice. Something about his voice and manner seemed familiar.

She opened her eyes and glanced up at him again. Something was wrong. As she tried to figure it out, she noticed a dark spot on his face that was mostly hidden from the mask.

She glanced at his hands. A tattoo protruded from his sleeve and a memory returned... she'd seen that tattoo on the man who'd attacked her at her house. The height and build were right—and that mark on his face was right where he'd be bruised from her elbow.

He caught her eye just as she realized he wasn't a nurse. Too late.

He jerked the pillow from behind her head and shoved it over her face, cutting off her air supply. She gasped as he pressed the pillow harder. She kicked and struggled but he'd climbed onto the bed and used the full leverage of his body to hold her down.

She flailed for something to fight back with but there was nothing. Her fingers clawed into his skin but her body was growing weaker and weaker with each passing moment.

She was going to die.

"Get off her!"

Josh's voice reverberated throughout the room. Suddenly, the man's weight was gone. She shoved the pillow off her and gasped for air as the two men scuffled. Josh pulled his gun but the man managed to knock it from his hand. She scrambled to find the button to alert the nurses or the phone to call for help. Her throat was raw from the lack of air and she wasn't certain she would be able to even voice a cry for help, but she would do what she could.

She crawled onto the cold concrete floor as they continued to fight. The gun that had been knocked from Josh's hand had slid beneath the bed. She scrambled to reach it, relief flooding her when she felt it in her hands.

She pushed to her feet. Josh and the assailant were still tussling. She couldn't get a clear shot of the guy without possibly hitting Josh. She wasn't sure she had the voice to yell but she raised the gun. "Hey!" she called out. Her voice was barely a whisper but they heard her and both turned.

The assailant gave Josh one last push, then took off running from the room. She couldn't fire, not without the threat of hitting an innocent bystander.

"Go after him," she said, pressing the gun into Josh's hand. "Go."

"Are you okay?" She nodded instead of speaking and waved him away.

He hurried out the door.

Cecile stumbled toward the bathroom. She turned on the faucet and let her hand catch water. She sipped from it, wincing from the rawness of her throat.

She stared at herself in the mirror and spotted the redness around her mouth and neck. There would be bruising there for certain. As the adrenaline rush passed, she felt her strength fading. She managed to make it to a chair by the bathroom door before her knees gave out completely.

It seemed like hours ticked by before anyone returned. Josh darted back through the door and rushed to her, two nurses following him inside.

He'd lost his cowboy hat and a gash on his forehead above his eye was trickling blood. He also struggled to catch his breath after his scuffle, yet all his attention was focused on her. "Are you okay?"

Once again, she nodded instead of speaking. Her throat burned and speaking only made it worse. But she had to know. "Is he…?"

His breath hitched again and he slowly shook his head, a disappointing weariness covering his expression. "He managed to get away from me but I've alerted security and phoned the team to get down here to investigate. I didn't get a good look at his face. Did you?"

She frowned, then shook her head. She

hadn't really seen his face, either, thanks to the mask covering it. But therc had been one distinguishing mark. "He had a tattoo on his arm. It protruded out from under his shirt. I didn't get a good look at it."

"Maybe we'll catch a break and get a good image of him on the security cameras."

She hoped so. This guy apparently had no qualms about getting close to her in public places. He'd taken a big risk coming here, talking to her, letting her see him. True, she couldn't identify his face, but he'd showed himself. That was brazen. And he'd broken away from his usual methods to try to kill her—something serial killers hated to do. That indicated he might be fixated on her for some reason—enough to come after her multiple times, in many different ways, rather than moving on to another, more vulnerable, victim.

Josh stroked her face. "I thought I'd lost you when I came in and saw him," he whispered, his voice choked.

She leaned into his touch. He very nearly *had* lost her.

"She needs to get back to bed so we can do a thorough check on her," one of the nurses insisted, interrupting their moment. "And you should get that gash looked at, Sheriff."

At first, she wondered if he even heard the nurse. His focused seemed lasered on her, but he finally nodded. He helped her to her feet but her knees immediately buckled. He responded by swooping her up into his arms and carrying her.

She sucked in a breath at the feeling of his arms around her and the strength of his muscles and shoulders. It felt good to have him be there for her. He placed her on the bed, then let the nurses hover over her trying to reattach her IV that had pulled loose.

He cleared his throat and found his voice. "I should go check with the security team and see if they found anything. I'm also going to arrange to have a security guard posted by your door. This man will not get to you again." He gave her hand a squeeze of reassurance before nodding to the nurses then walking out.

She jumped at the sting of the needle as the older nurse—her name tag read Paula—reinserted her IV. "You had quite a scare," she commented to Cecile.

"I guess I did."

"I can't believe this happened here," the

younger nurse, Maggie, said, turning away. Her voice was low but frightened. "If he attacked you here, nowhere is safe."

Paula tried to shush her but Cecile heard the fear and desperation in the young woman's voice. She was scared and she had a reason to be. Somewhere out there, a killer lurked in the streets. Tonight, he'd found his way into this very hospital. He'd been hunting women in the area for years. And it was only a matter of time before he struck again. Right now his attention was focused on her but how long would that last? How long before he turned his sights on someone else? Or before he finally managed to kill her? She shuddered at the thought.

Paula did her best to reassure her. "Sheriff Avery won't let anything happen to you. I've never seen him like this." She turned away. "I'll send someone in to clean up this mess."

"No, don't." Cecile didn't want anyone else, someone she didn't know, in her room around her. She couldn't risk it. Sure, the hospital was now on high alert but she wasn't at her best. She wouldn't be able to fend off another attack. He'd proven that. He'd very nearly succeeded in killing her today.

Paula seemed to understand her fear. "No

problem. We'll take care of it ourselves."
She squeezed Cecile's hand and shot a look
at Maggie, who frowned. Cecile was sorry to
add to their workload but she didn't want to
be caught off guard again.

She leaned back in the bed and tried to
settle her racing heart and catch her breath.
It still unsettled her that the killer had gotten
close enough to strike.

Too close.

Thankfully, Josh had been close by as well.
Josh had swooped in to rescue her. Again.

She thought she'd witnessed his true feelings for her, but now that the moment had
passed, she felt less sure. Cecile knew he
cared about her. But would he ever be able
to take a risk on her—and on love again?

That was the question she still didn't know
the answer to.

Josh hung up his phone as he spotted Greg
and Zeke hurrying toward the hospital's security office.

"How is she?" Greg asked.

He saw worry on both their faces and understood it. This wasn't just any other victim.
They all knew her and cared about her. She

was one of them and that upped the anxiety level.

"She seems to be okay for now."

"Your text said she was attacked again. What happened?"

"I walked into her hospital room and he was on top of her, holding a pillow over her face. We fought but he got away." He still couldn't believe he'd allowed that maniac to get away from him. "I've got the chief of security pulling up the video cameras. I'm hoping they captured an image of him."

"Do we think this is the same guy that attacked her at her house? The serial killer we're currently investigating?" The horror of Zeke's question hit them all hard.

As much as he wanted to deny it, he couldn't, any longer. "Yeah, we do. He's got his sights set on Cecile now. I didn't have the opportunity to tell her but Joe Thomas confirmed someone attached a canister of nitrous oxide to the air-conditioning system on her truck. That crash was no accident. He was trying to weaken her to make it easier to get to her."

Zeke and Greg shared a worried glance, then looked back at him. "What do you want us to do?" Greg asked.

"We've got two tasks. Get those security images so we can search for anything to help us identify this guy, and keep Cecile's room secure so he can't get back in."

"Plus, you need to have that gash looked at, Josh. It might need stitches." Zeke pointed to the wound on his forehead. It was bleeding like crazy but wasn't his biggest concern at the moment.

"I'll stay here and light a fire under the head of security," Greg suggested. "Why don't you go to the ER and have that taken care of? Looks like you might need stitches."

Zeke agreed. "I'll walk you down to the ER, then stay with Cecile until you get finished."

That was the best plan he could think of, so he acquiesced.

It felt good to know he had people he could count on. Greg had long been a trusted deputy and Zeke, who'd also recently become his brother-in-law, was growing into a fine deputy as well.

Josh wouldn't admit it but he was starting to feel a little off balance, probably from blood loss, on top of everything else he'd been through in the past few hours. He'd changed the gauze already several times, having gotten some from the nurse on duty when he left Cecile's room and stuffed it in his pocket.

Zeke got him settled into the ER and a nurse started cleaning his head wound.

"We heard what happened upstairs, Sheriff. Are you okay?"

"I will be."

"Is it true there's a serial killer in the hospital?"

"We don't know that," Zeke told her. "Someone attacked Deputy Richardson but we have no proof yet that he was looking to attack anyone else or that he has any prior history of violence."

Josh couldn't help smiling at that response. Admit nothing but do his best to calm the situation. Cecile had taught him well.

"Well, I hope you catch him soon. I've been watching the news and the serial killer is all they talk about."

He didn't like hearing that but he couldn't control what the news stations chose to broadcast. If he could, he would delete himself from their news for good.

"It's their job to create a climate of fear," Zeke told her. "That way, you'll keep tuning in to catch the latest updates. I'd ignore anything except for official statements from the sheriff's office."

"I'm sure you're right." She patted Josh on the back. "Let me go grab a suture kit. I'll be right back and fix you up good as new."

He watched her leave, then turned to Zeke. "That was good."

"Yeah?" The kid looked to him for confirmation and he liked being able to give it. He'd always liked Zeke but he'd come to admire him more after the way he'd stepped up when Josh's sister Kellyanne was in danger. Not only had he taken steps to protect her, he'd built a family with her and made her and the rest of the Avery clan very happy.

"Why don't you go on up and make sure Cecile is okay. And ensure the security details are in place. I don't want her room unguarded again. She's still weak from the previous attack. She needs time to rest and gather her strength."

Zeke nodded and walked out.

The nurse returned after a moment and stitched him up quickly, giving him six stitches. "You probably won't even have a scar, Sheriff, but if you do, it'll be something to be proud of. You got it in the protection of someone you care about."

"Yeah, I did." It felt good to admit that. Not that he was surprised the nurse had known he had feelings for Cecile before he'd said anything. Courtland was a small town. Everyone knew everyone else's business. Still, he felt his face warm at the mention of it. He wasn't ready for that part of his life to be on display.

"I need you to lie down and rest for fifteen minutes so we can make sure the meds aren't going to affect you."

He nearly protested but decided to lean back and do as he was told for once. He felt better knowing that Greg and Zeke were taking care of things. Being sheriff meant he often delegated responsibilities. He was used to it. But this felt personal, and he knew he wouldn't have been able to hand over Cecile's safety to anyone but the men he trusted most.

He placed his cowboy hat on his chest and tried to relax but his mind was a rush of information overload and his heart was still hammering. He glanced to the outside wall and spotted the TV on, broadcasting the interview Cecile had given the day they'd found the Jane Doe.

She looked so strong and so formidable as she vowed the sheriff's office wouldn't stop until they brought this killer to justice. It was a far cry from the woman he'd had to carry back to her bed, holding her close in his arms. No wonder people thought something was going on between them.

There is, though, isn't there?

He closed his eyes. That situation was also murky. He dreamed about holding her, loved spending time with her. *Face it, Josh, you're crazy about her.* And yet he couldn't quite bring himself to take their relationship to the next step. Not when he knew that progressing any further would lead to the ultimate letdown in the end.

FIVE

Cecile had never been one to stay still. She preferred to be active. And that meant that staying home and resting once she was released from the hospital felt like wasted time. She had a killer to find before he struck at her again or, worse, at another innocent victim.

She flashed back to the feelings of helplessness and fear that had overwhelmed her when her assailant had her pinned down under the pillow. She hadn't been able to fight back. She'd been arrogant before in the belief that she'd always be able to defend herself, but he'd proven her wrong. She rubbed her jaw. It still ached. She was regaining her strength every day but that memory would haunt her forever.

Josh wasn't happy to see her when she showed up for her shift at the sheriff's office but he hadn't sent her home. She actually thought he was glad to have her around even if it was just so he could keep a closer eye on her. Whatever his reasons, she was thankful. Not only did she feel safer at the sheriff's office, but she could also focus on something other than her own fear and pain. She still had a serial killer to track down.

She added her name and photo to the board displaying this serial's known victims. She hadn't been murdered but he'd definitely made her his target.

The task force deputies welcomed her back before updating her on what they'd found while she was out of commission. The canister and the attack at the hospital seemed very different from what they knew about his other attacks. He was taking risks that seemed out of character.

Perhaps it was time to readjust the profile they'd started to put together for him.

"We noticed previously that his disposal methods had changed over time."

Marla nodded. "Yes, he seemed less concerned with his victims being found in his later murders than his earlier ones."

Greg continued, "You theorized that he was likely getting bored."

"And arrogant," Cecile insisted. "He's lost

the fear of getting caught. He's even escalated to public attacks—proven by his attack on me at the hospital."

"He still took precautions, though," Deb Miller pointed out. "He wore a mask and avoided showing his face on the security cameras." Greg had gathered that information from the security tapes and it confirmed that while their guy was getting bolder, he wasn't without discretion.

"He's looking for a challenge," Chet Cartwright, a deputy from Shaw County, threw out, then glanced at each of them to see if they'd criticize or confirm his theory.

Cecile reexamined everything they knew about this killer. "You might be right, Chet."

Her encouragement seemed to embolden him. "You set yourself up as the ultimate challenge, Cecile. The night your department found that Jane Doe, you did that press conference with the news stations and assured the public you would find this guy. He might have taken that as some sort of a taunt. That might be why he's suddenly fixated on you."

Her heart fluttered with both fear and excitement. This explained a lot. Only, if it was true, he wasn't done coming after her.

Her cell phone buzzed and she glanced at it.

It was a text from Dr. Joyce Brewer, the medical examiner, alerting her that she had something for them. Cecile hoped it was something that would move their investigation forward and help identify their killer.

She quickly responded that she was on her way. "This was good work," she told the group. "Keep going. I'm heading over to the medical examiner's office. She has some information about our Jane Doe."

She rapped on Josh's door and explained about the text. He immediately stood and grabbed his hat. "I'm coming, too."

"That's not necessary." Logically, she knew it was probably safer for her to have backup, especially since the killer seemed like he could strike again at any moment. But still, she didn't like the way Josh looked at her now—like she was broken and needed his assistance. Even if that was just her pride talking, she found it hard to let that go. Sometimes, it felt like pride was all she had left.

"You shouldn't be driving yet. Your reflexes aren't back to their best."

She gave a resigned sigh. "Fine. You can come, too."

She climbed into his truck and buckled up for the drive to the medical examiner's office.

They weren't a big enough department to have their own ME, so their district contracted the work to a physician in another county.

They made the forty-minute drive with no problems and greeted Dr. Brewer.

"What do you have for us?" Cecile asked her.

"Quite a lot." She motioned them toward an examination table at the back of the room. "For starters, she was strangled and stabbed. That's consistent with the other victims' injuries. However, these remains are at least a decade old."

Cecile's pulse increased. That was older than any of their known victims. "She could be the first victim of our killer."

"And if she was the first victim, she was probably someone the killer knew and spent time around." The excitement in Josh's tone and face was evident. He was as enthused about this finding as she was. This might finally be the key they needed to point them to the killer's identity.

"Have you been able to make an identification yet?" Cecile asked.

Dr. Brewer nodded. "I was able to match dental records with a missing-person report filed ten years ago. Our victim's name was Erica Littlejohn."

Erica?

Cecile swallowed hard, then felt the room spin. It was too much. She hadn't dared get her hopes up. Hadn't even allowed her mind to go there. She'd searched for so long and now this was all that was left of Erica.

Josh's arm went instantly around her and she clung to it.

"What's the matter?" Dr. Brewer asked.

She couldn't answer. Her voice was paralyzed from shock.

Josh answered instead, his face grim and his tone flat. "Cecile knew her."

The doctor frowned. "I'm sorry."

This was the day, the moment, she'd been waiting for. She'd searched for years trying to find out what had happened to Erica, thinking and believing that if she could only find her body, she would have answers to all her questions. She'd imagined being glad for the closure. But she'd never imagined the sick feeling retching through her at the sight of her best friend's mangled remains and the knowledge of the terrible things that had happened to her.

She'd finally found her friend.

And finding Erica only raised more questions.

Josh was amazed Cecile was still standing. He kept his arm around her, partly to keep her steady but also so she would know she wasn't alone.

He led her to a chair, giving her time to process the shock. Good thing he'd come with her. He'd hate to think of her learning such news without anyone there who'd understand what this meant to her.

He turned back to Dr. Brewer. "Is there anything else you can tell us that might help the case?"

"Not much. The bones themselves are in good shape, but there isn't much forensic evidence left after all these years. There also wasn't anything special about the tarp she was wrapped inside." She handed him a folder. "Here are my official findings. I hope they help you catch this guy." She glanced at Cecile. "I'm sorry about your friend." Dr. Brewer stepped away, giving them some time alone.

Cecile's eyes remained locked on the remains on the table. "Do you want a minute?"

She dabbed at tears forming at the corner of her eye, then stood. "No. I said my good-byes a long time ago. I want to catch this guy."

Her determination amazed him. She was so strong even as the hits kept coming one after another.

As they exited, he walked by her side just in case she lost her footing again—but that didn't happen. They reached his truck and both climbed inside. She was quiet on the drive back to Courtland and he was comfortable giving her that space.

"I always suspected she died that night," she finally said. She kept her eyes focused on the landscape rolling by them. "I told myself over and over that she'd died that night. However, I suppose a small part of me always believed she'd be found alive."

"You had hope."

She nodded, then gave a weary sigh and turned to him. "That's gone now."

"At least you know." It was a small comfort but at least it was something.

"No more searching Henderson's fields." She gave a strained laugh. "He'll be happy about that, at least."

"You were right, though, Cecile. She was

probably buried there in that grave on his property."

"Somehow being right doesn't have the same satisfaction I thought it would."

The pain in her expression broke him. He reached across the seat for her hand and she let him hold it. He didn't know how else to help her now except to find the person responsible for the murder. "At least this gives us a starting point. Finding Erica's remains changes things for the investigation, Cecile. We now know that our serial was at the graduation party that night. You've spent all this time investigating Erica's disappearance. You might have already found evidence that points us to him without even realizing it."

"But I never had any leads that went anywhere."

"Because you were looking for a missing person, not a killer. Now we have a clearer picture. I'm going to keep the others working those task force leads but you and I should go back through your notes about Erica's disappearance piece by piece. The killer's identity must be in there somewhere."

She nodded and he could see the shock beginning to wear off. Knowing her, he was sure that renewed determination would soon replace it. She'd dedicated her entire adult life to finding Erica. Now she would refocus that to finding her killer.

But, for now, she still looked so haggard and fragile. He didn't want to push her into something she wasn't ready for. "Maybe you should take another day to rest."

"My day of rest could lead to someone else being attacked. I want to find this guy before he hurts anyone else, Josh."

He smiled at the determination in her tone. That was the Cecile he knew. And it was the Cecile he needed right now. "Call the station and tell them. We'll head right to your house and get started. There's no time to lose."

She placed the call to the others and even emailed them a copy of the medical examiner's report. Josh trusted them to work the leads and he was sure Cecile did, too, but this new information was something he and Cecile could best address together.

He pulled into her driveway and parked. She stiffened beside him and it occurred to him that she might be afraid of this house now—or at least of being there alone. Some maniac had broken in and stolen her peace of mind.

Well, she wasn't alone any longer. "Let me

check inside first," he said as they got out and approached the front door.

If he needed proof that she was still reeling from the shock of discovering her best friend's body, he'd have found it in the fact that she didn't even argue. He cleared the house, then ushered her in and locked the door.

"My office is small and cramped. It probably won't be comfortable for the two of us back there. Why don't you start moving boxes into the living room while I make us some coffee."

That was a good suggestion. They might need the added room to spread out. He moved several boxes to the living room and also brought out her evidence board, basically a corkboard with a mishmash of photographs attached.

Once he was done, he glanced around at all the information she'd collected over the years. Ten years' worth of work borne from her dedication to her friend, which might finally lead them to the killer.

"You think I'm weird for having all of this stuff, don't you?" She carried two mugs of coffee as she walked into the room.

He took one, then shook his head. "I don't think so at all. It speaks to how much you cared about your friend."

"I couldn't give it up. I knew the answer about what happened to her was out there somewhere. I just didn't know how to find it. That's why I decided to become a cop—to learn the skills to figure it out."

"This is going to help us, Cecile. Ten years is a long time. Memories fade and evidence gets lost. Your work has captured some things that might not have been around to collect any longer if not for you."

She set down her coffee cup and slid into a chair. "Erica's mother died never knowing what had happened to her daughter." She glanced at the photos pinned to her evidence board. "For weeks after she vanished, I scoured social media for photos from the party. I tried to piece together who was there and figure out a whole timeline of what they did that night and who they were with at what time."

That had been smart of her. Most of these images would now be lost to closed social media sites or accounts.

"It was mostly local kids plus a few from neighboring counties. Mike Mulligan—do you remember him?—he was living in a mobile home on a patch of land bordering the Henderson Ranch. He threw the party. We were just a group of kids drinking and celebrating the ending of one part of our lives."

He scanned some of the images. "Cecile, I'm seeing a lot of familiar faces here."

"I know that. A lot of people were at that party that night, Josh, including several of the Avery brothers." She pointed to photographs of Josh, Miles and Colby. They'd been a few years older than Cecile and the other graduates, but that hadn't stopped them or others from showing up at a party.

"So now you think me or my brothers could have been involved in Erica's disappearance?"

Her faced reddened but she smiled. "Of course, I don't but I didn't know any of you then. I couldn't leave any stone unturned."

"So you ruled us out?"

"I spoke with some girls who vouched for Miles and Colby's whereabouts and, apparently, you and Haley were joined at the hip back then."

Ten years ago, he and Haley would have been newlyweds. It seemed odd now that they'd attended a high school graduation party, but they'd been so young back then.

"I've ruled out all the females—they all either had someone to vouch for their whereabouts or lacked the physical strength to overpower Erica. I also managed to rule out several of the guys based on interviews with the women who were with them that night. I placed a star on their pictures."

He'd noticed the stars and was glad to know what they meant. Of course, women had been known to lie for men sometimes and Cecile hadn't exactly been a seasoned law enforcement veteran when she conducted these interviews, but it was a good start.

Still, there was no way she'd managed to pinpoint everyone who was there. "You don't really know the names of every person who was at the party, though, do you? There could have been people there that you didn't know or just didn't see. As I recall, it was a free-for-all kind of night."

"It was. I've gathered all the names I could based on who I remember being there, who I could identify from photographs, and who other people described as being present. But you're right. Anyone could have shown up. There wasn't exactly a guest list."

"So we should start by questioning people who were there—showing them this list and asking if there's anyone who was left off."

"You want to reinterview people? Ten years later?"

"I do. This is now a murder investigation and these witness statements are our best chance at figuring out who was there and who saw what. It's been years since you last spoke to them. It's possible, with enough time, people will recall something they'd forgotten or didn't think was relevant when they just thought Erica was missing. It's also possible they'll be more likely to talk now than they were then. Relationships change. Someone who knows our killer may not have the same loyalty to him that he or she did ten years ago." That was often the way cold cases became hot again.

"Where do we even start?"

"The same place you started ten years ago." He pulled out a list of names of people she'd interviewed. "We'll start with Bryce Henderson. Do you remember why you interviewed him first?"

She pulled his photo from the array. "Bryce was the first person I suspected when I realized something might have happened to Erica. He'd been asking her out for months and she kept turning him down. She thought he was creepy. I knew he was there that night and no one I spoke to could vouch for his movements. He, of course, denied even seeing Erica that night and became very agitated when I started questioning him about her. I kept up with him through the years and discovered he had several sexual assault accusations against him at college that all got swept under the rug, probably by his uncle's money. He's always been my number one person of interest."

Josh knew him. Frank Henderson had taken in his nephew after he was orphaned in a car wreck when Bryce was twelve. The kid had grown up so spoiled and entitled that Josh had no trouble believe everything Cecile was telling him. Frank had spent half his life building his fortune and the other half spending it to bail his nephew out of trouble.

"I haven't seen Bryce in years. He didn't return to Courtland after college, did he?"

"Not that I'm aware of. As far as I can tell, he's moved around a lot, but thankfully, he liked to post about himself on social media, which let me keep tabs on him. The last known address I found for him was in Mexico. That was several years ago. After that, he vanished. If he returned to Texas, he's been keeping a low profile."

"Well, his uncle would have the means to keep him hidden. Let's call Zeke and have him run another background and criminal check on him. For now, I want to head over to Henderson Ranch. Frank surely knows where he is—and hopefully, he can be convinced to tell us. If he's stepped foot in Courtland at all in the past ten years, I want to know about it."

She nodded and made the call.

Josh gathered up all the information she'd collected on Bryce Henderson. Despite his less than stellar behavior, nothing in his movements indicated he'd been in their area to commit these murders. Still, at least they had a lead to check out.

It was possible all they had to do was follow the trail of clues she'd constructed and it would point them to the killer.

Talking about her investigation had helped center Cecile, but reopening all these memories only reminded her of that terrible night. If Bryce Henderson lived under the radar and killed all of these women, she knew that it would make her sick to know she'd had him in her sights all those years ago and had failed to build a case against him, leaving him at large to hurt so many others.

Josh pulled the truck into the entranceway of Henderson Ranch. He stopped at the security gate and asked to speak with Frank. The security guard made a phone call as she and Josh waited.

"Do you think he'll see us?" Cecile asked him.

"He doesn't have a choice," Josh reminded her. "This is now a murder investigation and we have very good reason to believe that the body was buried on his property. He'll answer my questions until I'm satisfied he didn't know anything about it."

She admired his bravado. He wasn't afraid to face any situation head-on. Usually she wasn't, either, but the attacks, along with the shock of learning Erica's fate, had shaken her. She was glad he was beside her to make certain nothing went overlooked.

The security guard hung up the phone and pushed a button that opened the gate as he waved them through. Josh parked in front of the house and they got out and walked to the door. Frank met them and ushered them both inside.

"Morning, Sheriff, Deputy Richardson. What can I do for you today?"

Looking around, she noted that his house was large and spacious. She also noticed several men huddled around the fireplace and glanced at Henderson.

"Members of my security detail," he explained, motioning to the men. "We were in the middle of a security meeting when you called from the gate."

Josh didn't let their presence stop him. "We've identified the body that was removed from your property, Frank."

The head of security—Kennedy—interrupted. "It hasn't been proven that that body was ever buried here."

Cecile shot him a glare. What was he, a lawyer now?

Frank waved him away. "Thank you, Kennedy, but I think it's safe to say she probably was." He turned back to Josh and Cecile. "You have an identification. Who was it?"

Cecile answered. "Erica Littlejohn. She went missing ten years ago during a graduation party near your property line. Your nephew Bryce was at that party."

His arched his brow at his nephew's name. "Bryce? I recall him being questioned about a girl's disappearance at the time but he didn't know anything about it. To my knowledge, he didn't even know her."

"Well, that's just not true," Cecile insisted. "I happen to know he asked her out several times and she turned him down each time."

Henderson didn't flinch. "Is that so?"

Josh stepped in. "We're reinterviewing witnesses in this case. We would like to speak to him about the graduation party that night but we don't have a current address or phone number for him. I'm sure you, as his uncle, know his whereabouts and how we'd be able to get in touch."

Frank hesitated a moment before answering. "Unfortunately, that won't be possible. Bryce died eighteen months ago of a drug overdose."

Cecile felt her heart drop. She shot Josh an incredulous look and saw he was just as surprised as she was by this disconcerting news. If Bryce had been dead for eighteen months, he couldn't be responsible for the attacks against Cecile.

"He was down in Mexico working on my behalf. He'd always been a little too into the party scene and struggled with addiction for years. It finally killed him." Frank gave them the specifics—the date of Bryce's death and the city where it happened. Josh jotted down the details in his notepad and Cecile knew he'd be checking into them later, just to verify.

After that, there wasn't much more they could do but mark him off their list. They'd tied Erica's death to the serial killer and Bryce couldn't be that guy.

"Thank you for your help," Josh said, then turned to leave. Cecile followed him, devastated. She'd been so certain Bryce had been involved in what had happened to Erica.

She was nearly to Josh's truck when she spotted a an approaching figure, whom she recognized as Tom Rainer. They'd attended school together and Tom used to work for her father on his farm.

He smiled as he approached. "Hi, Cecile. Sheriff, good to see you again. What are you doing here?"

"We had a few questions for Mr. Henderson about his nephew. Unfortunately, we were too late."

"Oh, yeah. I heard about him dying. Henderson flew down there last year to take care of his affairs. I think losing his nephew really hit him hard. That was the only family he had left."

"I didn't know you worked here," Cecile told him. Tom attended her church, so she saw him fairly frequently, but they were friends only in passing. In fact, she couldn't really remember the last time she spoke to him other than to say hello.

"Kennedy hired me two years ago. It's a good job even if Henderson is a little paranoid."

Cecile crossed her arms and leaned in close to him, intrigued. "Paranoid? What do you mean by that? Is it connected to why he has such a large security detail?"

He saw her interest and straightened, seemingly realizing that he'd said too much. He shot a worried look at Kennedy, who was exiting the house and heading his way. "I really can't talk about that, Cecile. I could lose my job."

Kennedy bellowed out his name. "Tom! Do you have those reports I asked you to retrieve?"

He held up a sheaf of papers. "Got 'em."

"Then let's get back inside. I'm not paying you to stand around chatting."

"See you later," Tom said, hurrying toward the house.

Cecile nearly let him go then remembered Tom's name had been on her list—he'd been at the party, too. "Tom, wait!" He stopped and turned to her. "I need to ask you a few questions. Official business," she shouted at Kennedy, who was shooting arrows at them with his eyes.

"What's going on?" Josh asked her.

"This is Tom Rainer."

Josh nodded. "I remember. We met the other day."

"Well, Tom is on my list. He was at the graduation party the night Erica went missing." She turned to Tom. "Weren't you?"

"Well, yeah. Everyone was."

"Do you remember seeing Erica Littlejohn that night?"

He narrowed his eyes, thinking. "She was the girl who went missing, right? I don't really remember. In fact, I don't remember much of anything from that night. It was a long time ago—and I spent most of the party getting drunk with Mitch Hopper and his crew."

The mention of Mitch Hopper sent waves of embarrassment through Cecile. She'd put herself out there that night hoping to impress Mitch, only to be shot down. If Tom had been with Mitch and his friends, he would surely have seen that.

She cleared her throat and tried to regain her composure even though Tom had hit a nerve. She pulled on all her years of professionalism and reminded herself that she had to push through. She owed it to Erica to find her killer and stop a madman from preying on her town. "Do you recall seeing anything out of the ordinary? Any faces you didn't recognize?"

"I don't think so, but like I said, I was kind of out of it, especially by the end of the night. I woke up the next morning at my grandad's old service station and no idea how I'd gotten there. It was a wild time."

That didn't surprise her much. Mitch and his friends had been drinking quite a lot at the party. Nearly everyone had. On the plus side, it was possible Tom had been so drunk he didn't remember her faux pas with Mitch.

"Thanks for your help, Tom. It was good to see you again."

"You, too, Cecile. See you at church on Sunday."

"Everything okay?" Josh asked her as they headed for his truck again.

Tom's mention of Mitch Hopper had her red-faced with humiliation. The thought that she was going to have to dig into the past and relive memories she would rather forget hit her. She didn't want to go there, but she was going to have to in order to paint a full picture of her own whereabouts at the party—and why she hadn't been there for Erica. Sooner or later, Josh was going to ask, and he'd need to know the truth.

Even if it was the last thing she wanted to tell him about.

"Sure, fine. I just realized this trip down memory lane isn't going to be pleasant for me."

"Investigating a murder never is."

"Yes, but this is my past, too, Josh. I'm just not looking forward to speaking to all of these people again. That terrible night was one I would rather forget altogether but I can't, can I?" She sighed and climbed into the truck.

Josh slid in beside her and gave her a curious look. "Something has you rattled. Was it that Tom Rainer? Did he say something?"

"No. He just reminded me of something I would rather forget." She really didn't want to discuss the whole Mitch Hopper fiasco with Josh, but better that he hear it first from her. Mitch was on the list of people to question and he was sure to bring up what had happened between them that night.

But as much as she tried to steel herself to force out the words she needed to say, she just couldn't manage to do it. She wasn't ready to share that with Josh yet. Instead, she changed the topic, motioning to the group of security personnel huddled together. "For a second, I thought Tom was going to tell me what Henderson needs with all this security, but then Kennedy interrupted him."

Josh stared at the group, then started the engine and took off. "That's too bad. I've been wondering about that myself."

Josh shared Cecile's concerns about the security at Henderson Ranch. He understood Henderson had a large ranch to protect, but protect from what? And why hire such a large team? He'd known of bigger ranches hiring a ranch manager and hands to help with the cattle, horses and upkeep, but the more he saw how this security team functioned, the less they seemed like normal ranch workers. They wore suit coats and gun holsters and not one of them looked like he'd done manual labor in years. Kennedy looked like ex Special Forces and the whole team had gotten tactical training from Paul. Why would any of that be necessary on a normal working ranch? And where *were* the usual ranch hands—or animals, for that matter? The only people he ever saw around were Henderson and his security team.

He'd have to remember to talk to his brother about his observations and maybe do a thorough background search into Henderson and his men.

Cecile looked shaken in her seat, probably at the news about Bryce. Josh didn't remember him really, but it was clear he'd rubbed Cecile the wrong way. She'd seemed certain that he was a good lead—but it had just been a dead end after all. It was time to move on from him. "Was there anyone else you suspected of being involved?"

"I picked up on Bryce early on but I still did my due diligence with others. No one else stood out to me, though."

"Okay, then we start reinterviewing everyone else. Who was the next name you had?"

She picked up her list to check. "That would be Caitlyn Murphy."

"Why'd you start with her? Do you remember?"

"Caitlyn was our graduating class's busybody. She kept her eyes open for everything that was happening. I knew if anyone had seen Erica go off with someone, it would have been her. Only, unfortunately, she was too preoccupied with her boyfriend that night to see anything."

"Okay, then. Let's find Caitlyn and see

what she remembers about that night. Her recollections might have changed."

She took out her phone and looked up Caitlyn. "She's an attorney for a law firm in Dallas. It's over an hour's drive. Are you sure you want to make it today?"

"If you're right, she might be able to shed some light on the night of the party. That's worth a couple of hours of our time. However, it wouldn't hurt to look through that list and see if there's anyone else on it that's in Dallas. We might as well speak to as many people as we can while we're there."

She nodded and started going through their list.

When they stopped for gas and Cecile went to use the restroom, he pulled out his phone to call his brother about Henderson. Although also Cecile had questions about Henderson's need for so much security, he knew that her focus was on Erica's case and he didn't want to distract her with another investigation that might be a wild-goose chase. They already had enough on their plates.

Paul answered with a "Hey, what's up?"

Cecile would return soon, so Josh knew he didn't have time for small talk. "I just left Henderson Ranch and something about that place seems fishy to me. Did you get any vibes when you were there for your training session?"

"Sort of. It was the first time I've ever done a tactical training mission for a ranch's security team. I didn't notice any signs that it's even a working ranch. No trucks, farm equipment or signs of cattle or horses."

"That's what I found odd, too. I've heard rumors that Henderson is buying up all the land he can get his hands on but he doesn't seem to be working it. Any idea what might be going on?"

"Nothing good, I'm sure. You want me to dig into Henderson?"

Josh nodded as he noticed Cecile returning. "Let me know if you find out anything." He ended the call, then climbed back into the truck and continued on toward Dallas.

GPS directions led them toward a twenty-story office complex. Josh pulled into the parking garage, parked and got out.

Cecile smoothed her hair and clothing and seemed more nervous than he'd ever seen her while conducting an interview. "What's the matter?"

She bit her lower lip, proof of her anxiety. "I don't know. It's been ten years since I've seen Caitlyn. She works in an office building and, based on the cars in this lot, probably makes more money in a month than I make in a year."

Josh grinned at her nervousness. It seemed very out of character for his usually calm and collected deputy. "I'll see about getting you a raise," he teased, hoping to make her laugh. But all she did was take a deep breath— something he knew she often did to settle her nerves. "Don't worry. It'll be fine."

However, once they stepped off the elevator and into the offices of the firm where Caitlyn worked, he had to admit to feeling a little out of place himself. The décor in the waiting area told him this law firm's rates were something neither he nor Cecile could ever afford. If Caitlyn was a lawyer here, she was doing very well for herself. He wasn't one to be intimidated by wealth but he was a simple cowboy who felt a bit out of his element.

Josh flashed his badge at the receptionist and asked to speak with Caitlyn Murphy. The receptionist told them to take a seat in the waiting room. Cecile sat but kept fidgeting as if she couldn't stop the restless energy that was pouring off her. Josh could only hope that this interview would lead to something useful, to make up for the fact that being here was clearly making Cecile miserable. According to Cecile's notes, Caitlyn hadn't had anything useful to share when she'd been questioned ten years ago, but there was always a chance she had remembered something, anything, since that previous interview. After all, they were no longer investigating just a missing person. Erica's case was now a homicide. People tended to take it more seriously when there was proof the person hadn't left on their own.

The receptionist called their names and motioned for them to take the hallway to the last door on the right. They didn't have to worry about where they were going. Caitlyn stood outside her office door. Josh didn't remember her right away, but when she spoke, it came back to him. She'd been a rodeo queen like Haley, only several years younger.

"Well, well, well, Sheriff Josh Avery. As I live and breathe. To what do I owe this visit?" She put her hand on her hip and played up an accent he was certain she only used when it suited her. If a partner passed by at this moment, it would likely vanish as quickly as it had appeared.

"Actually, we're here on business, Caitlyn. You remember Deputy Cecile Richardson?"

She turned her gaze briefly to Cecile. "Of course. Hello, Cecile. How are you?"

"Hi, Caitlyn. It's nice to see you again. Mind if we talk in your office?"

"Come on in." She motioned for them both to enter, then closed the door behind her. The office was large, with a great view and beautiful furniture, proving that Caitlyn was doing well in her profession.

After they both sat, she rounded her desk and took a seat in a chair that raised her above them slightly. It made her look important and Josh was sure that was the intent. "What can I do for the Courtland County Sheriff's Office? You certainly are a long way from home."

Cecile took out a notebook that contained her notes. "We're here to ask you about the night of the graduation party. The night Erica Littlejohn went missing."

Caitlyn rolled her eyes. "That again? Really, Cecile. You're still looking for her after all these years?"

Cecile's expression hardened and she stiffened in her seat. Caitlyn had hit a nerve and suddenly Cecile's certainty and resolve were restored. "Actually, no, we aren't still looking for her. Her body was discovered dumped into a shallow grave. She'd been bound and murdered." Her words were curter than she'd probably intended but Caitlyn's dismissive tone had diminished Erica's importance. That wasn't acceptable.

Josh placed his hand on top of hers in an effort to help her keep her cool. "We're investigating a murder now, Caitlyn. The evidence indicates that Erica Littlejohn was killed the night she vanished. Someone at that party knows something, so we are reinterviewing everyone that was there."

Caitlyn's face shifted from shock to horror to what looked like sincere sorrow. She leaned back in her seat and turned to meet Cecile's eyes. "I'm sorry. You have my condolences."

Cecile nodded in response.

"I wish I could help, but I just don't think there's anything I know that would be useful. That was ten years ago. Plus, I drank a lot that night. Most of it is a blur."

Josh wasn't letting her off that easily. "I understand that, but the smallest detail really could make a difference, if you wouldn't mind walking us through what you *do* recall. For starters, can you tell me who you came to the party with?"

"I went with a group of friends but we all

separated once we arrived. I had my eye on a certain fellow and I went to find him."

"And what time did you leave?"

"I don't know. Like I said, I drank a lot. I don't really remember anything past the first hour or so. I woke up the next morning in my bed. I have no idea how I got there. My friends didn't know, either."

Cecile picked up the questioning. "What about people you saw there in that first hour? Do you remember who all was there? Do you recall any altercations, anyone arguing, or someone that didn't belong?"

Caitlyn thought for a moment, then shook her head. "I'm sorry. I don't."

Josh saw real sincerity in her demeanor. She wasn't just putting them off or covering for someone. Josh noticed Cecile's shoulders slump. Caitlyn really didn't know anything. They'd hit another dead end.

Cecile thanked Caitlyn, then stood to leave, but she was too kind to end their visit on a bitter note. "It's nice to see you're doing so well for yourself."

Caitlyn smiled. "Thank you. I've worked hard to make something of myself. Leaving Courtland was the best decision I ever made. I'm surprised you're still there, Cecile. I always thought you'd lcave town the moment you had the chance."

He glanced up in time to see Cecile's cheeks redden. "I might have if it hadn't been for Erica going missing."

That was when he realized why she'd been so nervous. She was confronting a woman who'd done what she hadn't—gotten out of Courtland and made something of herself. Cecile had remained primarily because of her loyalty to Erica and her driving need to finding what happened to her. Now that they knew, Cecil's choices were wide open.

He thought about what Sheriff Milton had told him.

Everyone wanted Cecile on their team. She'd had multiple job offers.

And there was nothing else holding her in Courtland.

SIX

Cecile and Josh interviewed several other former classmates who lived in Dallas. None had any more information to offer than Caitlyn. Apparently, a night of drinking and partying—along with a decade of time passing—had wiped out a lot of people's memories.

Of course, no interview could be as bad as the one with Caitlyn. Cecile couldn't believe how that woman had flirted with Josh with Cecile standing right beside him. She always had been a flirt. It had been like they were back in high school all over again and Caitlyn had her eye on every guy that came along. And Josh hadn't seemed the least bit bothered by it, either. Why would he be? Caitlyn was still as beautiful as ever, plus an incredibly successful attorney to boot. Cecile had struggled to be civil but her father had taught her better manners than that. Besides, she really had been hoping Caitlyn might have remembered something.

Cecile cringed when she read the next name on the list—Mitch Hopper. She was dreading interviewing him. She'd forced herself to speak to him years ago when Erica first disappeared, but looking back at her notes now she knew that she'd probably been in too big a rush and way too emotional during that interview to dig for answers the way she should have. Thankfully, he hadn't appeared to notice.

They tracked Mitch down to the car dealership where he now worked in sales. It was an occupation that fit him. He had the charm and charisma to move big-ticket items and, of course, he was as handsome as ever.

Josh shook his hand. "How are you doing, Mitch?"

Of course, Josh knew him. Mitch had been a hometown football hero. He'd taken their team to the state championships. Everyone knew him. That only made her humiliation worse.

"Sheriff, Cecile, what can I do for you? I assume you're not here to purchase a truck… although, I could get you a great deal."

"No, we're actually investigating a murder."

"Murder? You mean those deaths I saw on the news?" He shot Cecile a leer. "I saw you on the news coverage talking about it. You looked good." He gave her a wink for good measure that made her blood boil with anger and her face warm with embarrassment.

He obviously remembered how she'd thrown herself at him that night and was continuing to poke fun at her.

He turned back to Josh. "Why are you coming to me? I'm in and out of Courtland all the time but I don't live there anymore. I only go there to see my folks. I'm not sure how I could be of any help with your investigation."

"The body we found last week turned out to be Erica Littlejohn."

"Whoa, she actually died?" Mitch asked, looking genuinely taken aback. "Man, I really thought she just ran off, like everyone said. So you're saying she was murdered? That's crazy."

"Right…well," Josh said, clearly trying to get the conversation back on track. He kept his tone professional, but she could tell he wasn't very impressed with Mitch. Cecile wasn't, either. What kind of jerk heard about a classmate being murdered and just said that it sounded "crazy"? "We believe she was attacked on the night of Mike Mulligan's graduation party. Do you remember that party?"

"How could I forget?" He shot Cecile a look, then another wink as he grinned wide. "You were smokin' hot in that dress."

Dread filled her. Of all the things he could have forgotten about that night, why couldn't it have been her throwing herself at him?

Josh shot her an incredulous look and fumbled to respond. "What—what does that mean?"

"It was the one and only time I ever saw this lady here in a dress and makeup." Mitch was enjoying this little trip down memory lane and Cecile was disgusted by his callousness, continuing to joke around even under these circumstances.

How could she have ever dressed up for this guy?

Mitch's behavior appeared the same today as it had ten years ago. He was still basking in his high school days while everyone else had moved on.

She shuddered. How *could* she have ever been attracted to this guy?

And all the while she was throwing herself at Mitch Hopper, she was letting down her friend, leaving her alone and vulnerable to a killer.

Her tone turned hard as she pressed Mitch to take the matter seriously. "I would think the most memorable thing would have been the girl that went missing at that party. Do you remember everyone talking about that? Someone who was there that night at the party was murdering her while the rest of you were guzzling beer and getting falling-down drunk."

He stuffed his hands into his pockets and had the decency to look a little embarrassed. "I didn't learn until the next day that she'd gone missing."

Josh returned the conversation back to the topic at hand—the investigation. "Was there anyone at the party that you didn't recognize?"

"Not that I recall. But then again, people were coming and going all the time. It was dark and I really did have a lot to drink."

Cecile sighed. That was becoming a common theme to this investigation.

"I do remember there were a lot of older kids there, like ones that had already graduated. It wasn't just our class—it was a come-and-go kind of party. I hooked up with Tracy and didn't really pay much attention to who else was there."

"Thanks for seeing us, Mitch." Cecile turned and walked away. She needed a shower now to wash the revulsion she felt at knowing she'd ever been attracted to this guy.

"No problem. Hey, you two come back and see me when you get ready to buy new vehicles. I'll give you an amazing deal."

Josh followed her back to the truck. She noticed he seemed off ever since Mitch had spilled the beans about her and the party. Well, if they were going to talk about this, she supposed it needed to happen now.

She stopped and stared at him. "What? What's wrong?"

He rubbed his hand over his head. "I just can't picture you and Mitch together. You actually liked that guy?"

"I was nineteen. I was stupid and immature." She put her hand on her hip and silently begged him to just drop it.

He did not take the hint. "But you dressed up for him?"

She threw her hands in the air, humiliation and frustration fighting for front and center in her emotions. "What do you want me to say, Josh? I wanted him to notice me as a woman, not as one of the guys. I thought changing my look would get his attention, but all it did was make him laugh at me. I put my heart out there, and it got stomped on. Lesson learned."

She walked to the truck, opened the door and slammed it again without getting inside.

Josh walked up behind her and touched her shoulders, a bitter reminder of another man who didn't want her. His voice was softer when he spoke. "What's this about? You can't really be that upset over Mitch Hopper not liking you ten years ago, can you?"

She pressed her hand against her face and tried to calm the storm of tears that threatened to burst through any moment. Finally, she shook her head. "It's not that."

"Then what is it?" He spun her around to face him, saw the anguish in her expression then pulled her into his embrace. She buried her head against his shoulder and choked back sobs.

"It's just that after Mitch rejected me, I was so humiliated I ran into the meadow where all the cars were parked. I found a place to hide and I spent the next hour crying my eyes out." He rubbed her back and she relished the feeling of being in his arms. "Then I went home, even though I'd promised Erica that we'd stick together. I left without her—left her behind to be murdered. We had promised to stay together, Josh, and I just ran off and left her there."

He forced her to look up at him. His eyes were kind and forgiving. "That wasn't your fault, Cecile. You weren't to blame for what happened to Erica."

"But if I hadn't left her alone—"

"You were a kid. It wasn't your fault."

He wiped a tear from her cheek but didn't move his hand away afterward. His finger outlined her face and caressed her lips. She leaned into it, loving the feel of his hands on her. They were face-to-face and it would take hardly any movement to close the distance from her lips to his. She didn't dare. He was the one holding back on ever being in a relationship again. He was the one who needed to make the move. But the hammering of her heart was screaming at her to kiss him.

His breathing grew heavy and he stroked her hair as the tension between them grew with each passing moment.

Then he broke it, stepping back from her. He forced a smile on his face that did its best to cover the tremble of his hands. "Or I could go get Mitch back for you. He seemed pretty interested in flirting with you."

Disappointment rushed through her. He was trying to be lighthearted and funny. She gave him a smile and tried her best to put behind them what almost happened, but the truth was that Mitch wasn't the only man who'd rejected her.

Josh didn't want her, either.

They drove back to Cecile's house in silence. The interviews hadn't thrown any new light on the case, so it was time to go back through everything else in her file.

Cecile had closed herself off from him since that moment in the parking lot of the car dealership when he'd almost kissed her. What had he been thinking?

He'd been thinking how pink her lips were and how soft her skin. He shook his head to clear it before it wandered back down that path. He couldn't go there and they both knew it. Not with this cloud hanging over him.

Once back at her house, they dug back through her files. After a while, she gave a weary sigh, then pushed the papers away. "I can't do this."

He knew he'd better tread carefully. "Do what?"

"I'm not used to working at home. I'd rather load these boxes into the truck and finish this at the office. At least there, we'll have the conference room table to spread out on. Plus, the task force team can help us sort through it all."

He leaned back. Her meaning was coming through loud and clear. She didn't want him in her private space like this. He guessed he should have expected that. "If that's what you want." She stood and stretched her neck, her hand rubbing the back of it. She turned to him again.

"Actually, no, it's not what I want but I think it's what's best. I can't keep going on pretending like nothing has changed between us. If you don't want me, that's fine, but I can't keep up this pretense."

He leaped to his feet. "Wait, what? You think I don't want you? That I'm not attracted to you?" He couldn't have heard her correctly. But her eyes shone bright with hurt and pain.

"I know you're not over Haley. And I know that nothing I do or say is going to make you look at me the way you used to look at her. I'm not what you want—I get it. We don't need to talk about it again."

"Cecile, I never wanted you to be Haley. I only ever wanted you to be you." He cupped her face with his hands to make certain she heard what he had to say next. "You are exactly what I want."

Her chin quivered and she pulled away from him. "You don't have to say that. I know that's not true."

"Oh, Cecile, I do want you. Believe me, I do." He struggled against the weight on his chest. Everything in him wanted to sweep her up into his arms and prove to her how much she was wanted. But he'd made a promise to himself. He wouldn't saddle her with his shame. "You know I've got this shadow following me around over Haley's death. I can't be with you because I don't want to drag you under that shadow, too, not because I don't want you." He stared at her, then reached out and stroked her chin. "Any man in his right mind would want you."

She stared at him and his words seemed to sink in. Suddenly, she looked up at him. "Are you telling me truthfully that that's the reason we can't be together? Because of those people who still believe you had something to do with Haley's death?" Her brow creased and she gave him an incredulous look. "Wait, are you serious? That's the dumbest thing I've ever heard. I don't believe for a second you killed Haley. Why would I care what other people think?"

He bristled at her comeback. "Maybe you

don't care now but what about five years from now? What about when our kids come home crying because someone called their daddy a killer? You'd grow to resent me. You might even start doubting whether I did it or not."

"That's ridiculous."

She was being shortsighted, refusing to see that them staying apart was for the best. "I'm sorry. I just can't risk it. Even for you," he told her, his eyes fixed on her. "Especially for you." He touched her face again, her soft skin and lips beckoning him to hold her, to kiss her. Holding her at arm's length was exhausting, but it was what he had to do.

He stepped away from her again, doing his best to maintain that distance. Doing otherwise wouldn't be fair to either of them.

He glanced at the papers and boxes that had invaded her living room. "I think you're right about taking all of this back to the sheriff's office. We're not making any progress here."

He loaded up boxes and carried them to his truck, then climbed inside. Cecile joined him without saying another word. She was quiet on the drive, too, probably still trying to work out a way to change his mind. It wouldn't happen. No matter how much he wanted her, he could never be with her. She was right about one thing. They couldn't continue on the way they had been acting, like nothing had changed between them.

It was time he put some distance between them once and for all, for her sake.

Diving headfirst into a killer's thought process was just what Cecile needed to do, to keep her mind off the situation with Josh. Things were weird between them. She wasn't a hundred percent sure she believed him when he said he wanted her, but she did know this insinuation about him murdering his wife had hung over him for too long. If she could solve Haley's murder, then he wouldn't be able to use that excuse any longer.

But she needed to concentrate on capturing this killer first.

Josh had dropped her off at the sheriff's office with the boxes of information then returned to his family's ranch. It was for the best. They needed some distance between them after their awkward confrontation.

She'd quickly started sorting through the boxes, trying to make sense of what she'd collected over the years. The interviews—both the old ones and the new ones from that day—hadn't shed much light on the suspect they were trying to find, except to verify that they weren't looking for a stranger. Not a single person had mentioned seeing a stranger or anyone who didn't seem to belong. This guy was someone known to them, someone local to town.

She opened several of her profiling books and started rereading them, hoping for some guidance to help her come at this investigation from a different standpoint. If the physical evidence wasn't going to lead them to their killer, she would have to rely on behavioral profiling.

She dug through her books on the subject. She stood back and tried to see the behavioral patterns of her killer. The problem was that his behavior seemed to be erratic and his patterns changing.

He'd blitz-attacked his earlier victims, catching them off-guard, indicating a lack of social skills with which to lure in his victims. At the beginning of his killing streak at least, he had perhaps been socially awkward and unable to express his feelings of anger. Given the typical backgrounds of serial killers, it was likely that he would have acted out against women even before his first kill, probably through instances of aggression toward women—stealing, stalking or harassment.

He might also have had a history of petty crimes and/or violence against animals. He was also smart—smart enough to avoid detection all this time and to keep law enforcement from realizing there was a serial killer at work until recently. He might have been smart enough to hide his early criminal activity, meaning there wouldn't be any arrest records for those crimes.

However, that kind of behavior wasn't the type people in law enforcement usually forgot. Any well-trained officer knew that someone displaying that sort of delinquency as a teen could escalate into more serious crimes in adulthood. It was possible one of the local sheriffs or police chiefs would remember someone who exhibited such behavior.

Based on when the murders began—ten years ago, with Erica—and the fact that everyone at that party was within a few years of Cecile's age, that meant she had a general idea of how old the killer would be now. Everyone had the party had been in their late teens or early twenties. Counting back, if their suspect had committed those acts as a child or preteen, that would have predated Josh joining the sheriff's department. He might not have any knowledge of the crimes, but his father might.

She picked up the phone to call out to the Silver Star, then stopped herself. It would be easier to explain her conclusions in person, plus the ride would help clear her head.

She removed her gun from her desk drawer and tucked it into its holster, then grabbed the keys to one of the sheriff's office cruisers. "I'm heading out to the Silver Star," she told Jamie, the night-shift dispatcher. "I have my cell phone if you need me."

"Okay, thanks, Deputy Richardson."

She climbed into the cruiser and headed to the ranch. Halfway there, she had second thoughts about visiting Josh's home after their conversation earlier but she didn't turn around. She had a legitimate reason for going to see Josh's dad. His insight could be critical to the case.

The moment she turned off the highway and drove under the sign that read Silver Star Ranch, barking dogs circled her car. Several stopped howling once they realized they knew her but it took a few of them a little longer to calm down. The porch light came on as she parked. Josh stepped out onto the porch. She got out and met him.

He gave her a smile that sent tingles through her. She had to stop letting him affect her that way. He'd made it very clear he wasn't interested in moving forward with a relationship. Maybe she should have just used the phone instead.

"Come on in," he said, flashing her that lazy smile of his that made her go weak in the knees.

She stepped inside. It felt like home being in this house. His parents had always welcomed her and made her feel like part of the family.

Mrs. Avery hugged her. "You're just in time. We were about to sit down to supper."

"I don't mean to intrude," Cecile insisted.

"Nonsense. You're always welcome here," Mr. Avery reminded her. "Take a seat."

She looked to Josh and he gave her a nod, so she sat down.

"How are things going with you staying here?" she asked him, knowing that since his cabin had burned down a month ago, he'd moved in temporarily with his parents.

"It's fine."

"Any plans to rebuild the cabin?"

"I don't think so. We built that for me and Haley. I don't see any reason to rebuild for just me."

The air in the room seemed to still at the mention of Haley.

Mr. Avery quickly steered the conversation away from the subject. "Josh tells me you were chosen to head the serial killer task force. Congratulations. That's quite an accomplishment."

"Thank you."

"How's the investigation going so far?"

"Honestly, not great. That's kind of why I came. I've been working on a profile for our killer, and I could use your help. I believe he is local."

"Based on what?"

"Well, we know he was at the graduation party where Erica was killed. Josh and I interviewed people we know were there and no one remembers seeing any strangers or anyone that seemed out of place."

"That makes sense."

But Mrs. Avery was shocked. "You mean it's someone we know?" Cecile understood the horror of that realization. No one wanted to believe that kind of evil could hide in a community where they'd always felt safe.

Mr. Avery turned to his wife. "People like this always live among us, Diane. They work in communities, shop, even attend church with us."

"As you know, most serial killers have a history of violence as a child. Animal killings, obsession with fire, petty crimes involving women." She glanced at Mr. Avery. "I was hoping you remembered someone with that kind of history. Someone who's around my age, who still lives in the area. He might not have had any charges officially filed against him but you may have received some complaints about his behavior while you were sheriff?"

He rubbed his chin as he thought back. "I can't think of anyone offhand but I have my notes stored in the attic. I'll pull them down and go through them. Something in them might jog a memory."

"Thank you. I'd appreciate that."

Josh turned to her. "We should also contact the other law enforcement agencies in the surrounding counties. I agree with your assessment that he's local, but not everyone at that party lived in Courtland County. People had friends or cousins who came in from further afield. Familiar enough not to stand out, but maybe not close enough to have landed on my dad's radar."

She nodded. "I'll do that."

They spoke of less heavy matters while

they finished eating. Mrs. Avery told her about a planned activity at church. "We're opening a food and clothing pantry to the public one weekend a month. I've already had several people offering to help with collecting food and clothing."

Cecile felt bad. Her job rarely gave her the opportunity to commit the time to volunteer like that, but she wanted to do what she could to help. "I probably have some clothes I could donate."

"That sounds wonderful. Thank you. I'll send someone by to get them."

Cecile excused herself after they'd finished eating. "I should be getting back to the office. I left Marla and Zeke working on a timeline of our victims."

"How is Zeke doing with his first task force?" Mrs. Avery asked.

"He's doing fine. Your son-in-law is clever and thinks outside the box. That'll serve him well."

Josh stood, too. "I'll walk you out."

She thanked the Averys for the meal and Mr. Avery promised to let her know if he found anything in his notes.

At the door Josh reached for his hat, then followed her outside and down the front porch steps. "I'm glad to know your team is making some progress on this case."

"We're working every angle we can think of. It's such a daunting task. I can't believe this guy has been operating under our noses all this time."

"I saw on the news they're calling him the East Texas Strangler."

"So I heard. I thought you stopped watching the news."

He shrugged, as if it didn't matter that the local news stations, and especially Dirk Wilson, had targeted him every opportunity they got. "It's my job to keep up with what's happening in my county."

"Are you coming back to the station tonight?"

He shook his head. "No, I'll stay here. I want to help my dad go through those notes. You had a good idea there. How come you didn't ask me, though?"

"You'd only just joined the department ten years ago, when Erica was killed. You wouldn't have been part of the department yet for anything our killer got up to in the years before that, when he was a child or early teen. Your dad is our best resource for that."

"That's good police work, Cecile. Really

good. It's no wonder Sheriff Milton and the rest of them wanted you to head this task force. I agree with them that you were the best choice. I'm glad you're on my team."

She smiled at the compliment. It felt good knowing he valued her work as an investigator. She just wished he valued her as more than that, too.

He pulled out his cell phone. "I'm tracking the car until you make it back to the station."

"You don't have to worry about me, Josh. I'm feeling fine. I've got a secure vehicle and a gun at my hip. No one is going to mess with me."

Still, he didn't relent. "My middle name is worry."

"I thought it was David."

He finally gave in and slid his cell phone back into his pocket. "Text me when you get to the station."

She nodded her agreement before she climbed into the car and backed up. As she pulled from the long driveway back onto the highway, she checked in with Jamie to let her know she was on her way back.

The dark road ahead sent her thoughts to Josh and what she was going to do about her feelings for him. She cared so much for him despite their strained relationship. She didn't want to lose him as a friend, but she wasn't sure she could keep going the way they had been, either.

Headlights blinded her as another car sped up from behind her with their brights shining. She held up her hand to block the glare from the mirrors. Suddenly, the car rammed into hers. The jolt shocked her, especially when the car didn't speed away. Instead, it bumped her again, this time hitting her at an angle that seemed designed to push her off the road.

This was an attack.

She hit the speed dial button on her phone to call Josh. He answered on the first ring. "Did you make it—"

"I'm under attack," she told him. "A truck, black against red, two miles from Silver Star. He's trying to force me off the road."

"I'm on my way." She heard him run from the door and hop into his truck.

But the call had distracted her at the crucial moment, and before she could return all her attention to driving, the attacker managed to push the front end of her vehicle off the road, right into the embankment. The next thing she knew, she was flipping over and over again until the vehicle landed hard upside down.

The pain of the impact jarred her, sending her senses spinning. She spotted the truck stopped up the embankment, the headlights still shining. Then she heard the sound of the door slamming shut.

Her breath hitched. She had to get out of here. He was coming after her.

She struggled to move, only to find her foot pinned. She wasn't going anywhere. She reached for her gun at her hip but found the seatbelt in the way. She tried hard to unbuckle it, her hands shaking. She took several deep breaths. She had to pull it together. This guy was on his way here to kill her and she was *not* going to make it easy for him.

His boots crunched the leaves on the ground as he approached the car. She finally managed to free her gun and braced for the confrontation.

The moment he showed himself, she was taking the shot.

Josh had the sirens going and the lights flashing as he raced toward Cecile's last location, berating himself all the way. Why had he let her go alone? He'd known she was being targeted, had known that the killer could strike again at any moment.

If he'd managed to run her off the road, he was getting more reckless.

The light from his headlights broke through the darkness and came upon the scene. A truck was parked on the side of the road. He spotted the police cruiser overturned in the ditch and his heart raced. But it was the figure in the grass that caused his heart to stop.

The man had clearly been headed toward Cecile, but when he heard the siren, he turned and dashed back up the embankment toward his pickup.

Josh threw his truck into Park, grabbed his gun, then pushed open his door and hopped out. "Sheriff's Office, freeze!"

The man didn't hesitate. He sprinted toward the truck, dove in and took off.

Josh grabbed his radio and called in the make, model and tag number to dispatch. "Put out a BOLO for that truck and send an ambulance now. Cecile might be hurt."

He slid down the embankment and surveyed the damage. "Cecile?"

"Josh!" Relief flooded her voice and filled his own heart when he heard she was conscious and alert. "I'm okay—but my foot is caught. I can't get out."

He tucked his gun away, then leaned over

and glanced into the overturned car. She looked disheveled from the crash, but as she'd reported, she didn't seem to have taken any serious injuries.

Her face was pale, no doubt from fear. She holstered the gun in her hand. "Did you scare him away?"

He nodded. "He bolted the moment I pulled up."

"You should have gone after him."

He didn't tell her his first thought—his only thought—was for her safety. "I put out a BOLO for the pickup and radioed dispatch to alert the patrols."

He could hear the siren of the ambulance on the way. She scrunched her face. "You called for the bus?"

Her tone annoyed him. Of course, he'd called for the ambulance. "For all I knew, you were seriously injured in this car. You did just flip it, remember."

Her face reddened. "He came out of nowhere and overpowered me before I could speed away."

He leaned back on his heels as the realization of that comment hit home. "He was waiting for you. He followed you."

She gave a slight nod to indicate she'd had the exact same thoughts.

The firefighters and paramedics arrived and scrambled down the hill. Josh moved out of the way as they managed to free Cecile's foot and carry her up the embankment to the waiting ambulance.

"I'm not going back to the hospital," she told them. "My foot is fine. It was only caught, not injured."

One of the EMTs checked it out, probing and prodding. "It doesn't appear to be broken but we should still perform an X-ray. With the adrenaline in your system, you might not feel it if there's an injury."

"I'm fine," she insisted. "I don't want to go to the hospital. If it gives me any trouble then I'll come in and have it checked."

Josh bit back a tinge of annoyance at her refusal to be looked after, but he wasn't surprised. She never wanted any fuss over her—and she didn't like for people to see her when she was feeling weak or vulnerable. He noticed the way her hands trembled. She'd been shaken by the incident. "I'll drive her home," he told the paramedic.

He arranged for the tow truck and forensics team to arrive to clear the scene before they left, then placed a deputy in charge of making sure everything was overseen. He didn't expect to find any forensics that would lead them to their assailant but they had to cover all their bases. At most, they'd get some footprints from where the attacker had approached her car—but they had those already from the attack at her home, so it was doubtful this would yield anything new. As for the truck, they had the license plate, but given how careful the man had been up to now, the vehicle was likely stolen or using false plates. He'd run the plate number, but he doubted it would lead to anything. Still, he would let the team do their due diligence. You never knew when something unexpected would pop up.

He walked to his truck, where Cecile was already waiting. She was putting on a brave face but he could see she was in pain, if not from her injured foot then from the jolt of the wreck. She'd be feeling sore muscles tomorrow for sure.

"I don't want to go home," she told him when he climbed behind the wheel. "Take me back to the office."

"Cecile, you've just been in a car wreck. You need to go home and rest."

She bit her lip as she turned to look at him

and her voice was low. "He knows where I live, Josh."

He leaned back in his seat as those words sank in. This man had already attacked her once in her house. She'd fought him off that time but she was in no condition to do so if he showed up again tonight. She was right. Her home was not an option.

"Back to the Silver Star, then. You can stay the night in one of the spare rooms."

"Are you sure there's room with everyone home?"

Both Colby and Brooke and Miles and his family were staying at the main house, but it was a big house that had housed him and all his siblings. "There's plenty of room."

She agreed to go and he turned the truck around and headed home.

He longed to pull her into his arms and tell her everything would be fine, but that wasn't a promise he could make. Nor could he reassure her that he'd keep her out of harm's way from now on. Her safety was more important to him than anything else but they both had a duty to the public to find a killer.

There was no safety for her until this man was caught.

SEVEN

Cecile awoke the next morning to the sounds of the Avery house. As expected, she was feeling the aftereffects of the wreck this morning. She stretched to work out the kinks in her muscles, then dressed and walked downstairs.

The kitchen was bustling with people. All the Averys in one place including wives, husbands and children. Cecile wrangled Brady, Kellyanne and Zeke's oldest, as he ran past her. She swung him up into the air. He squealed with laughter right about the time her back squealed in pain.

Josh reached for Brady and set him down on the floor but he immediately took off again. "He's heavier than you think."

She gave him a nod, grateful he wasn't pointing out the pain he had to know she was in. "He's growing up so fast. They all are."

"How did you sleep?"

"I slept well." It was the truth. For the first time in a while, she hadn't worried about keeping up her guard for fear of someone breaking in in the middle of the night. She loved her house but it seemed less secure each day. The solitude she used to enjoy had started to feel menacing.

She smiled again as she took in the scene in the kitchen. The room was packed with Averys of all ages and sizes, bringing a sweet kind of chaos to the production of breakfast. Seeing them all together reminded her of how well they fit as a family—and how she didn't belong, no matter how warmly they'd welcomed her. She would never be a real part of this family.

Josh took her arm and nudged her outside. She followed him to the front porch, where he fell into the porch swing and motioned for her to join him. When she did, he slid his arm over the back of the swing and leaned in close to her. "You can stop putting on that front, Cecile. I know you're not fine."

Tears pressed against her eyes. He knew her so well. "I just love how busy the house is when everyone is home."

"It's busy, all right."

He tried to act like it annoyed him, but she

saw through his act. She nudged his shoulder. "You like it."

"Yeah, I guess I do. But it's sad, too. If Haley had lived, we would probably have a kid or two running around in that craziness."

It surprised her to know he thought about things like that. She'd assumed he'd tamped down those kinds of thoughts about what he was missing after Halcy's death. "I know what you mean. I spent so much time obsessed with Erica's disappearance while most of my friends were getting married and having babies. I sort of feel like I've missed my chance."

He looked down at her, his face unguarded and serious. "You haven't. There's still plenty of time for you to have all that."

"Does that go for you, too?"

He pushed back a strand of her hair, then breathed a weary sigh. "I wish it did."

She let his words sink in. He would never be married again, never have kids or a family. Not as long as he held to his resolve not to "burden" anyone with his reputation. She bit her lip to keep all the emotion threatening to burst through back at least until she was alone.

Then she got angry. "What is this, then? Why are we out here talking and swinging together?"

His eyes widened at her question but his guard went up. He didn't have to answer. She knew the truth. He was attracted to her but his excuses would keep them apart forever. He might never get past his own issues to make a life with her.

He stood, awkwardness now between them. "I'm heading to the office. You should stay here and get some rest. I'll come get you in time for the anniversary party."

She nodded and watched him walk to his truck. He had the ability to give her everything she'd ever wanted—hope, love, a family—yet he continued to deny her any of it.

The front door opened as Josh drove away. Brooke joined her outside, holding a plate loaded with food. "I brought you some breakfast."

"Thank you but I'm not hungry." She turned and hurried back into the house and up the stairs to the safety of the spare bedroom. She wanted to cry but the tears wouldn't come. Anger pushed itself to the forefront. She was tired of fighting her feelings. Either Josh wanted her or he didn't. And despite what he said, it appeared he didn't.

A while later, someone knocked on the

door. She quickly wiped away her tears and turned around. "Come in."

The door opened and Brooke stuck her head inside. "You okay?"

She nodded, realizing she owed Brooke an apology. "I'm sorry about earlier on the porch. You did a nice thing making me a plate and I was so rude."

Brooke waved away her apology. "I don't care about that. I'm worried about you." She and Brooke had become friends last year when she'd come to Courtland to find answers about her missing cousin.

"I'm fine. Really." But Brooke didn't move. She wasn't going to fall for Cecile's evasions.

Cecile fell onto the bed and groaned. "I'm just tired. I feel like I've been on this back-and-forth ride with Josh for too long. I'm ready to make some changes in my life."

Brooke frowned at that and sat beside her on the bed. "I hope that doesn't mean what I think it means. Colby says Josh is crazy about you."

"He has an odd way of showing it." She felt her face warm but wasn't sure if it was from anger or embarrassment. "I know Josh has feelings for me but he refuses to act on them. And nothing I can do will ever change his mind."

Brooke looked pensive for a moment, but then her face brightened. "I have an idea." She hurried out of the room and returned a few minutes later carrying a blue evening dress. "What do you think?"

She didn't immediately understand what Brooke was asking. "What do I think about what? Your dress?"

She smiled brightly. "Nope. *Your* dress." She pushed it toward Cecile. "To wear to the anniversary party tonight."

Now Cecile got her meaning. She stood and waved her hands. "I can't wear that. It'll leave you without a dress."

"Don't be silly. I couldn't decide between two outfits, so I brought both. You would look amazing in this dress. Especially with your hair done up and makeup and heels."

"No, no." She'd done that whole routine once before with Mitch ten years ago. She wasn't going to make a fool of herself again. "I can't."

"Why not? If you want Josh to change his behavior then you need to get him to see you in a new light. I guarantee you'll knock his socks off in this dress. Maybe that'll finally be enough to get his head straight about the kind of relationship he wants with you."

Panic gripped her at the idea of opening herself up that way again. "I—I can't."

Brooke spread the dress and shoes onto the bed. She looked disappointed but not angry. "I'll just leave this here. I hope you change your mind. If you really want to know how Josh feels about you, I think you should try every option you've got. Don't you want to know for sure before you move on?"

Brooke gave her one last look before walking out and leaving her alone.

She stared at the dress on the bed. It was beautiful but could she ever put herself out there that way again? She took in a deep breath, reminding herself that she wasn't that awkward teenager she'd been ten years earlier. She was a grown woman with a decade of experience and confidence. Why then did she still feel like that humiliated girl who got her heart shattered?

But Brooke was right. She couldn't walk away from everything she longed for with Josh without one last try. If nothing else, the dress would surprise him—and that might be enough to get him to drop his guard.

Josh got ready for his parents' anniversary party at the sheriff's office. He showered and changed into a nice suit he'd purchased for the occasion, then took one final opportunity to go over protocols with the deputies who were going to be on duty. Generally, he was always available if they needed to contact him, but he didn't want work to interfere with his parents' big night.

Colby entered the sheriff's office looking dapper himself—but then his brother was used to wearing a suit and tie for his job with the FBI.

"What are you doing here?" Josh asked him.

"I was sent over to pick you up so you wouldn't be late."

Josh bristled. "I'm perfectly capable of getting to the venue on time on my own." He turned to Marla, who was heading the dispatch line this shift. "Call me if you absolutely need to but try not to need me."

Marla smiled and assured him they would take care of anything that came up. With him, Cecile, Greg and Zeke all taking off to attend the anniversary party, Marla was the sole deputy in charge. It was a big responsibility, but he had no doubts she was capable of handling it.

Josh walked out to Colby's SUV. "Where's Brooke?"

"She and Cecile went ahead with Paul, Shelby, Lawson and Bree to help make sure everything was set up."

Josh frowned and checked his cell phone. He wished Cecile had waited on him or at least sent him a message letting him know she was going. On the other hand, he knew she didn't owe him an explanation.

"She'll be okay," Colby assured him, obviously seeing his irritation. "Paul and Lawson are with her. Nothing's going to happen to Cecile. Besides, that is one lady that can take care of herself."

"I know she can, but this time she's being personally targeted, Colby. This serial killer seems to have become obsessed with her. Just look at what happened to her last night. She's got to start being more careful."

"I agree it's a dangerous situation. I wonder, if it were anyone else, would you be so concerned?"

Josh shot him a glare.

Colby chuckled. "Why can't you just admit it, Josh. You're crazy about her."

"That's not what this is."

"It's exactly what this is. You're straddling the fence. It's time to make a decision. Look, I loved Haley and you two were great together.

But being sad forever isn't what anyone would want for you. And you and Cecile are good together. If you let her go, you'll always regret it."

Josh rubbed his face. His brother didn't understand. "I know I'll regret letting Cecile go, Colby. I'm prepared to live with that because I know it's what's best for her. It wouldn't be fair to her to develop a relationship when this suspicion that I was involved in Haley's death continues to hang over my head."

"No one who knows you believes you had anything to do with Haley's murder. In fact, a majority of the county elected you as sheriff twice. You're letting this one newscaster and a handful of people who agree with him keep you from moving on with your life, Josh. You can't continue to allow fear to rule you. That's no way to live."

Josh knew he was right, yet he couldn't seem to let go of the fear that Cecile would grow to resent him.

The anniversary party was being held on the Jessup property. They'd converted an old barn into a wedding and event venue. Strands of lights hung over the outside of the barn and plants had been placed for decoration. Colby pulled into a long, dirt driveway and parked in an area they'd marked for parking. The lot was already full. He checked the time and realized the starting time had already passed. He and Colby actually were late. They got out and headed inside where he could already hear music blasting through speakers.

Inside, they'd created a dance floor, added more lights and cleared an area on one end for catering, tables and chairs, and another area for music. He spotted his parents already mingling with guests and it did his heart good to see the smile on his mom's face. She looked to be enjoying herself.

Colby moved past him and pushed through the crowd to find Brooke. Both their faces lit up when they found each other and he pulled her to him for a kiss. They looked happy. So did Paul, Miles, Lawson, and Kellyanne, each with their own families. All his siblings had found love. He had to admit he was a little envious as he watched them all. He'd meant what he'd said to Cecile earlier. He wanted a wife and a family and everything he'd lost when Haley was taken from him. He could envision that happening with Cecile. It would be so easy to love her and build a life with her—but he remained sure that that wasn't an option.

He glanced around the room. Colby said she'd come with Brooke, so she had to be here. His heart nearly stopped when he spotted her. She was wearing a dress and heels that accentuated the best parts of her body, and her hair and makeup had been done beautifully. He'd never seen like this but recalled her story about dressing up to impress that guy at the graduation party.

Was this for him?

Maybe his brother was right. It was time he stopped allowing one person, one news story, to dictate his life.

Cecile had hardly recognized herself earlier in the mirror in this blue dress and heels, with her hair fluffed and styled and four different kinds of makeup on her face.

A flood of memories roared back to her. Memories of the night Erica died and how she'd put herself out there only to be rejected. Suddenly, she felt like that young girl again who just wanted a certain boy to look her way—and to like what he saw—but she kept hearing the laughter from the boys the night of the party.

Boys.

She had to remember that was what they

had been. And that had been a long time ago. But no amount of logic could will the insecurity away.

God, I hope he likes me.

She felt foolish, like a little girl hoping the boy she had a crush on liked her back. She was a grown woman, for crying out loud. Why then did she still feel like that little girl?

She shook her head as she reached for an appetizer at the buffet table, then turned and scanned the crowd that had gathered over the past half hour since she'd arrived with Brooke and the others. She spotted Mr. and Mrs. Avery. They were all smiles as they greeted everyone and thanked them for joining in their celebration. She also spotted several of the Avery brothers and their wives, including Colby. Brooke had told her Colby was going to pick up Josh, yet she didn't see him. She took out her phone. Maybe he'd sent her a text saying that he was running late or had gotten a call about an emergency. If not, she would have to ask one of his brothers his whereabouts. She felt silly dressing up like this if he wasn't even going to show up to see it.

Then suddenly, she got the sense that someone was watching her. She glanced up from her phone and locked eyes with him across the room. He was dressed in a fancy new suit and his blue eyes shone at her as a smile tugged at his lips.

She put away her phone as he moved toward her. She abruptly felt on display and silly in her borrowed dress, barely resisting the urge to turn and turn and run before anyone could comment on her uncharacteristic look.

She tried to paste on a confident smile as he reached her. "Hi, Josh." She straightened his tie. "You clean up nicely."

He leaned in close, his hand caressing the bare skin of her arms and sending flashes of lightning through her. "Cecile, you're beautiful."

Despite the way her heart hammered, she struggled to catch her breath at his words.

He slid his hand into hers and pulled her with him. "Dance with me."

It wasn't really a request but she wasn't going to say no. She moved with him to the dance floor, where he slipped his arms around her and smiled big when her handbag bumped against his arm, revealing the weight inside it.

"Is that a gun in your purse?"

"Of course."

"I knew you would be carrying. When I

saw you in this dress, my first thought was to wonder where you put it."

"Your first thought?" She lifted her eyes to him in a silent challenge and his face reddened.

"Okay. Maybe not my first thought." He stroked her cheek with his thumb and then outlined her face. "I'm glad you came." His voice was low and husky, full of emotion.

It was a moment she'd dreamed of, where he finally felt free enough to open up to her fully. "Me, too."

She pressed into his embrace and placed her head on his shoulder as they slow-danced. This was where she wanted to be, where she wanted to spend the rest of her life, in this man's embrace. She'd been aware of her growing feelings for years but now she knew how she felt with a certainty. She was falling hard for Josh Avery. She stared up into his eyes and saw her feelings mirrored in his expression and his little squeeze of her hand reassured her.

She didn't want this moment to end.

And it didn't…until gunfire lit up the room.

Josh pushed Cecile to the ground as he reached for the gun in his holster and scanned the room. His brothers had also drawn their weapons and taken what cover they could find. Cecile fumbled to pull her gun from her tiny purse.

"There!" Miles shouted.

Josh spun and saw a figure racidng out the back. He couldn't see the guy's face but there was no missing the rifle in his hand.

"Everyone stay down," Josh shouted as he quickly crossed the room, but he doubted anyone heard his command over the roar of crying and shouting that was filling the room.

The catering staff were also huddled on the floor but several of them motioned toward a back door, indicating the shooter had gone out that way.

Josh cautiously pushed it open and stepped outside. The intruder was nowhere in sight. He must have darted into the wooded area.

Moments later, Paul and Colby were beside him. "He came out this way. Let's spread out."

Colby went left, Paul went right, and Josh headed out straight ahead, hurrying through the parking area. This place was so far out that the shooter would have to have a vehicle in which to escape.

He scanned the area but found no sign of their shooter. He pulled out his phone, hoping for a text from one of his brothers that they'd captured him, but there weren't any messages waiting for him, so he hurried back toward the barn.

People were rushing out of the building. He spotted Cecile in the midst of the crowd, doing her best to keep everyone calm and orderly. She'd kicked off her heels and was in her bare feet. And that dress did a great job of accentuating her legs.

Stop it and focus on the matter at hand.

She locked eyes with him. "Anything?"

"No. I wasn't able to find any trace of him. Have you heard from Paul or Colby?"

"No, nothing."

"Why aren't these people inside where it's safer?"

"They don't believe it *is* safer inside—not after those shots were fired. We couldn't stop them from stepping outside, though we have managed to convince everyone not to drive off. We'll need their statements before they can leave."

The sound of sirens approaching was music to his ears. He needed extra bodies to search the area and also deal with the crowd—make sure no one wandered off and begin taking statements while the incident was still fresh in everyone's mind. They needed to question all the guests. The catering staff, too. Someone had to have gotten a good look at this guy. It couldn't be a coincidence that there was an active shooter at his parents' anniversary party, either. This guy was targeting Cecile and he'd followed her here.

He might not be able to convince all the guests to go inside, but he hoped he'd be able to get Cecile indoors. She was a sitting duck out here. "We need to get you back inside," he said, praying she wouldn't argue. "You're not safe out here in the open."

But Cecile was as stubborn as ever. "I need to help get everyone calmed down and start questioning people."

He pulled her close and leaned in to whisper to her. He didn't want anyone to overhear. They'd all just been through something terrifying. No use in letting them know the source of the danger might not be gone—and might, in fact, be looking for another opening to attack. "Cecile, you're a target. By standing outside with them, you're making everyone here a target. Has it crossed your mind that he created this chaos just so he could get to you?"

She glanced up at him, then gave a resigned nod.

She turned to go back inside as three more shots fired.

A roar of cries and screams filled the air. Josh pushed Cecile inside the building and pressed against the wall, covering her body with his. His heart pounded. He had a group of civilians that needed him but all he could think about was Cecile and keeping her safe.

They were close enough that he could feel her heart hammering. She stared up at him, her big eyes so wide and close. Her lips beckoned him. The way she fought to protect others amazed and infuriated him at the same time. She started to struggle against his hold. "Let me go," she insisted. "We need to check and see if anyone was hurt."

"Cecile, your being outside is putting all those people at risk."

"My being inside isn't helping to protect them, either."

"We've got deputies looking after the crowd and my brothers scouring the area for the shooter. We'll find him. But our priority has to be keeping these people safe."

He stepped away from her mostly to capture his breath. Being so close was just too tempting. "We need to start bringing people back inside. It's safer in here and we can control the room."

She nodded and started for the door.

He grabbed her arm. "Not so fast. Let the rest of us worry about that. You stay put. That's an order. You can start interviewing people once they're back inside."

He walked outside, glad to see that his family and the deputies were already doing their best to reassure everyone and usher them back inside.

This was bad. This guy had shot into a crowd with no regard to who might get hurt. His parents had been there. Children had been present. What did the shooter want? What did this accomplish? He didn't know.

He hurried and found his brothers. Paul looked disheveled and out of breath.

"Did you see him?" He didn't have to ask if he'd caught him. It was obvious he hadn't.

"He got away from me. He's fast. I didn't even get a good look at him before he disappeared into the woods."

Josh rubbed his face, struggling to push back his frustration so he could focus on what needed to be done.

He left his brothers and deputies to oversee another search of the parking area and perimeter. He helped usher guests back inside, assuring them they were safe in there. The crowd was scared but mostly calmed down once they were back inside and the doors were shut and the perimeter secured.

His father approached him. "What's going on? Did you find the man who did this?"

"No, Dad. We haven't. He got away."

"Is this the same man you've been looking for? The serial killer?"

"We believe so," Josh confirmed, "but I can't imagine why he would shoot into the crowd here. If he wanted to take her, it would make more sense to try to grab her when she was alone."

His father turned and scanned the crowd. "Or when there's chaos that he can blend into."

Josh saw where his father was going with his thinking. "He lured us out into the open." He'd had the same thought earlier.

He scanned the area, his heart full of relief when he spotted her reassuring two women and taking their statements about what they'd seen. It looked odd to see her without her usual boots and jeans but it didn't take away from her clear aura of strength and competence. She was as capable in a party dress and bare feet as she was in uniform.

He was crazy about her. He'd known that for a while now, and it was getting harder and harder to convince himself that he should push those feelings away. Maybe it was time to stop fighting with himself and let her know.

He walked over and she turned to him, all business. "Sheriff, this is Julia Stephens and Amanda Barker. They both claim to have gotten a good look at the shooter. I'm going to send them back to the office with Deputy Tyler to work on a sketch."

He nodded. "Good work. Thank you, ladies, for doing this."

Julia frowned and wrung her hands. "He looked so normal when he entered. I was working the catering table."

"Can you give a description?"

"Yes, he was tall, maybe six-two, with muscles and broad shoulders. He had a crew cut like you get in the military and I spotted tattoos on his arms when he reached for something on the table and his shirt and jacket pulled up. He was scanning the room like he was looking for someone. Then, he walked close to the door, pulled out his gun and started shooting into the air."

"Into the air?" Cecile asked. "Are you sure?"

"Positive. He shot several times up in the air, then started shouting for people to run."

Cecile turned to him. "He was trying to cause a panic. Why?"

Josh knew why. His father had been on the right track. "He was trying to create chaos. He probably thought he would be able to grab you without anyone noticing in all the hubbub." Everything about this guy was all over the place. He wasn't acting like a serial killer as much as an obsessed stalker. He'd gone off the rails. But why?

Either way, Josh was glad that whatever he'd been trying to do, he hadn't succeeded in getting to Cecile.

He motioned for Zeke to escort the ladies to the sheriff's office as planned. Hopefully the sketch they would generate would lead them somewhere or give them the break they needed to solve this case.

He took Cecile's hand and pulled her aside. "Take a walk with me." He couldn't wait another moment to talk to her. His insides felt like mush when she looked up at him with such anticipation and trust. "I wanted to say again that you looked so beautiful tonight."

Her face tinged red but she smiled. "Thank you, Josh."

"I realized that you were right. I've been hanging on to excuses for too long. I don't want to be without you anymore, Cecile. I want to take a risk and see where this goes."

Her eyes widened, then she smiled even bigger. "Are you serious?"

"Absolutely. You're my best friend, Cecile. Actually, you're more than that. You're the person I share everything with. I don't want to lose you."

She leaned into him and he wrapped his arms around her. She felt so right in his embrace. He should have told her so earlier. He touched her face, then covered her lips with his. No more guarding his heart. He was ready to be happy again.

EIGHT

Julia and Amanda provided a sketch, but unfortunately, it was too vague to really narrow down their search. She'd previously had one of the deputies on the task force follow up on the tattoo angle, but so far nothing had popped in that area. No one, not even her, had gotten a good enough look at the attacker's tattoo to adequately identify it. Cecile had asked the event planner if the barn had security cameras, only to learn that they'd never had need for them before. That didn't surprise her. She'd next approached the photographer the family had hired and he'd emailed her the images he'd taken. She was hoping to pick this guy out in the background of one of the photographs. If she needed to bring the ladies back in to look at them, she would do that, too. This was the first solid lead they'd had on this guy. She wasn't going to waste it.

She still didn't understand his reasoning. If he'd hoped to grab her while causing a scene, he'd wasted his chance. Thankfully, no one had been injured but poor Mr. and Mrs. Avery had had their special night totally ruined.

She glanced up and spotted Josh watching her. Her face warmed but it was a good feeling. He'd finally broken through his doubts and told her how he felt about her. That was a step she'd never expected him to take. She wanted to rush back into his arms but she had a killer to catch.

The phone on the conference room table rang and she picked it up. "Deputy Richardson."

"Did you miss me?" The voice on the line sounded menacing and mocking but she wasn't immediately concerned. They got all kinds of prank phone calls but usually not to her direct extension.

"Who is this?"

"You know who it is, Cecile. We've met before…multiple times."

Her blood ran cold as she flashed back to the voice of her attacker at the hospital. It was him. She was certain of it. "You're the man who attacked me in my home and at the hospital."

She glanced around but there was no one nearby whom she could ask to help her track this number. She quickly jotted it down from the caller ID, then cradled the phone between her ear and shoulder and texted Josh using her cell.

"I knew you would remember me. Don't bother with trying to track the ID. This is a burner phone and I'll be off the line before anyone can trace it to my location."

He sounded so smug and sure of himself that she itched to remind him how those meetings had ended for him but she bit her tongue. He was reaching out to her, which meant he wanted something. She needed to play along if she hoped to discover anything about him. "What's your name? What should I call you?"

"I like the name the TV is calling me. The East Texas Strangler. It has a nice ring to it. But you can call me Ted."

She saw Josh check his cell then look up at her. He jumped to his feet and ran from his office, grabbing the attention of everyone, including her team, who joined her in the conference room. Josh cautiously picked up an extension while the others scrambled to track the call. "All right, Ted, why are you calling me?" Cecile asked. "What do you want?"

"You."

His single word answer sent chills down her. Josh must have felt similarly because his jaw clenched at the caller's answer.

"Why are you doing this?"

"I saw you on the news. Your words were hurtful, Cecile. Very hurtful. I've tried to reach out to you several times but you keep thwarting me. I'm going to have to try a new approach."

She didn't like the sound of that. "What do you mean by that?"

"I've been watching you for a while now. I see how you care for people. You don't want to see anyone get hurt and you're always there to help those in need."

The more he spoke, the more dread filled her.

"If I can't get to you, there are others I can reach. You could stop me, Cecile. You vowed on TV that you would. Catch me before I kill again."

Her breath caught and tears welled in her eyes. She'd challenged him. That was why he was targeting her. "Are you saying you want me to catch you?"

"I don't want to go to jail and I won't be turning myself in, so forget about that. I'll keep killing until you do what you said you would do…catch me. You can end this simply by doing your job." He hung up, ending the call before they were able to trace it.

Cecile held the phone, continuing to listen to the dial tone as the line went dead. Fear filled through her.

"What did he say?" Marla asked.

She slowly replaced the receiver. "He said he was going to keep killing until I did my job and captured him."

Josh hung up his extension. "He's toying with you. Him reaching out only confirms what you suspected about him. He's bored and looking for a challenge."

He was right, but she wasn't keen on being that challenge. He'd also confirmed what Chet had said—that he'd locked on to her because she'd goaded him on TV. She'd been cocky and arrogant. He'd seen it as a taunt and he'd risen to the bait.

"As long as he's focused on me and not another woman, I'm fine with it. I can handle him. But now it seems like he'll be attacking other women just to rub it in my face." He might have been telling her a tale to get her riled up but she couldn't put anything past this guy and his erratic behavior.

"He's come after you several times now. I don't want to make that another time."

She shuddered as she recalled the helplessness she'd experienced at the hands of this maniac in the hospital. She hadn't liked the feeling of not being able to fight back. She had training, more than any of his other victims had. He liked them weak, liked to be able to overpower them, but she'd taken him down the first time he'd come after her. The second time, he'd caught her weakened by his previous attack.

She stared at the evidence board with all the faces of his victims staring back at her. He was coming after her again. She'd become a challenge to him. Maybe they could utilize that.

"No," Josh said when she turned to suggest the idea.

Her eyes widened in surprise. Had she mentioned it aloud?

"You don't have to say a word, Cecile. I know you well enough to sense what you're thinking and it is not going to happen. You are not going to make yourself a target just to capture this guy."

The others seemed to sense an argument brewing between them because they quickly ducked out of the room. Cecile was glad. It wasn't right to put others in the middle of this. Once they were gone, she stood and faced Josh.

"I'm already a target. He wants me. He's grown bored with his regular killings. He wants something more and he's latched onto me as a challenge. If he comes after me again and we're ready for him, we can finally capture him and get a killer off the streets."

He took off his hat and rubbed his head. "It's too risky, Cecile. Please don't ask me to let you do this."

She saw the worry in his face at her idea. She understood it, even appreciated it, but this plan could work. "Josh, what's more important? My life or bringing a killer to justice?"

"Don't ask me to make that call. Yes, arresting a killer is important, but so are you, Cecile."

Normally, she would have swooned that he cared for her that much, but today it irritated her. "You're too close to this. If it were anyone else, you would run with this idea."

He stood and gently stroked her arm. His voice was full of emotion as he responded. "But it's not anyone else. It's you. And I can't allow it." He walked out, heading to his office and closing the door.

She turned and watched him go, battling between wanting to scream with joy at his emotional breakthrough and wanting to scream in irritation that he was being unreasonable and emotional. How could she make him put aside his personal feelings and see that?

She sighed as she realized she couldn't continue to have it both ways.

She turned back toward her evidence board. She was going to have to find a way to capture this killer without putting herself at further risk.

How was she going to do that? She didn't know.

She pulled up a chair and stared at the board. There had to be something among all the clues they'd collected that would lead them to their killer. She had ten years' worth of interviews on top of what they'd collected from each scene. But where was the common thread? They could connect all these victims to one killer but the evidence wasn't leading them to a suspect. Josh's father hadn't been able to help them either. He hadn't recalled any kids who had fit the behavioral pattern Cecile had described, and his notes hadn't highlighted any either. She'd sent an email to the other law enforcement agencies in the vicinity but hadn't yet heard back from them about any names.

She spent the next few hours sorting through the most recent interviews she and Josh had conducted among people who'd been at the graduation party. She had a list of everyone she could document was there, and Zeke had created a database based on those findings. She pulled up that program and stared at the names. She knew it probably wasn't a comprehensive list. There could easily have been someone at the party that she hadn't accounted for but she could only work with the information she had for now.

A notification popped up on her email. She clicked on the photos from the event photographer at the anniversary party, praying for a break in the case. She spotted a figure that might be their guy but his face was hidden. These images would offer no solid identification. Another dead end.

She stared at the sketch Julia had provided her and thought about the details she'd mentioned, specifically the tattoos and military vibe she'd gotten from the shooter. She checked her database and saw only eight men from the party had gone on to serve in the military. It might be worth it to follow that lead and see where it took her.

She pulled up images of the eight men with military histories and printed out their photos. She would bring Julia and Amanda back in to see if they could identify one of them as the shooter, hoping their hunch that the shooter had been military wasn't misplaced.

Josh stared at the photo of Haley on his desk. He'd spent so many years alone after her death but he was finally feeling ready to move on. It was what she would have wanted for him. She wouldn't have wanted him to be alone.

He picked up her picture, stared at it for a moment and put it away in a drawer in his desk. He'd keep the picture safe, but there was no need to have it be the image he saw every day. He was ready to move forward with his life. He was ready to build a life with Cecile.

"I'm going to do it, Haley," he whispered.

He was tired of living half a life. He'd watched all his brothers and his sister find love and happiness with someone, and although he'd been thrilled for each of them, he'd sort of believed he'd had his chance and lost it. But now here he was, hoping for another chance at love, another opportunity to love again.

He hadn't planned to fall in love with Cecile, but she'd certainly made it easy to do so.

He spotted a group huddled around the TV and stepped out of his office to see what was happening. He saw Cecile on-screen. They were replaying her statement from the night they'd found Erica's body. He smiled again at her determination to find a killer and her assurance to the public that the sheriff's department was on the job, but he was reminded that this was also the interview the killer had viewed as her issuing a challenge.

"What's going on?" he asked. Cecile's clip surely wasn't enough to grab everyone's attention. They'd replayed that thing again and again.

"News of our serial has gone national," Greg told him.

The clip ended and Dirk Wilson appeared on the screen. "That was Chief Deputy Cecile Richardson alerting the public to a possible serial killer active in the area. The Courtland County Sheriff's Office is still asking for the public's help in finding the suspect. Twelve women have now been identified as victims of the East Texas Strangler. Several other homicides remain open, including the brutal murder of Haley Avery, wife of the now sheriff, Josh Avery. Her killer has yet to be brought to justice. This reporter, for one, feels the need to ask why this murder hasn't been solved and why her husband hasn't been further investigated."

Several people in the bullpen turned to look at him. Josh felt his blood boil. He was angry but he was also ashamed. Dirk liked to bring up Haley's murder and imply Josh's involvement every opportunity he got. This serial case gave him a lot of openings.

Marla quickly searched for the remote and changed the channel to another station, but surprisingly, this channel showed Josh's face in a box while a different reporter, this one from a national press, stood in front of the Courtland County Courthouse.

"There's breaking news coming out of Texas today. A serial killer known as the East Texas Strangler has been terrorizing several counties in east Texas over the past decade. Local law enforcement recently created a task force to find this serial killer but we're told these cases bring back memories of another unsolved murder in small-town Courtland, that of the wife of the current sheriff, Josh

Avery. Sources tell this newscaster that Sheriff Avery is still suspected by many to have been involved in his wife's murder. Meanwhile he heads the task force for a serial killer who has been operating in the area for a decade."

Josh wasn't sure if he was more shocked or horrified. He was used to being a target by Dirk Wilson from the local news, but this was nationwide. Now the whole country would think he'd murdered his wife. And he didn't have to wonder who this guy's source was for that information, either. Dirk.

Marla hurried to the window and glanced out. "There's three national news vans parked at the curb," she stated.

He turned and spotted Cecile standing in the doorway of the conference room, her arms folded and a dark look on her face. She locked eyes with him, pleading silently with him not to overreact. How could he not? This was the worst possible thing that could have happened. He'd like nothing more than to drive over to the TV station and confront Dirk, but he wouldn't. It wouldn't do any good. The damage had been done.

God, why does this keep happening?

It was engraved in media history now.

Every mention of the serial killer from now until the end of time would include a snippet with a reminder that Josh had not been ruled out for involvement in his wife's murder—with the implication that his involvement had somehow been covered up by the sheriff's office. It was a stain that wasn't going away.

The national coverage also had a chance to impact Cecile's reputation. She could be the face of this thing, winning acclaim for catching this killer—or she could have her name dragged through the mud if it was aligned in any way with his.

Cecile had her whole life before her. She was widely admired and valued for her investigative skills and her abilities. She could have a real future…unless she attached herself to him. This suspicion would follow him around until the day he died. And who wanted to hire someone who'd gotten romantically involved with a suspected killer?

Pinning her to him would place her future in jeopardy.

He knew what he had to do.

He had no choice left but to let her go.

Cecile followed Josh into his office. She felt sick at what she sensed was coming. She'd seen the change in his body posture, the sag of his shoulders as he watched the news coverage, and the disillusionment in his face when he'd locked eyes with her.

The distance he was now putting between them, both emotionally and physically, was obvious.

She closed the door behind them. No need for the entire precinct to witness this.

"Josh, please don't overreact to this."

"To what? My name and face all over the national news?"

"It doesn't mean anything. Not to anyone here."

"I know but it's out there, Cecile. It's being reported and filed as a story and every single time something comes up with the serial killer case, that story about me is coming up with it."

"So what? You and I and everyone who knows you understands that that accusation is false. Why does it bother you so much what other people think?"

"Because of you."

"Me? I don't care."

"I know you don't, but you should. You can still have a life, Cecile, a brilliant career. But you can't do that with me trailing behind you with this stain covering me."

"I'm not bothered by that."

"Well, I am."

Frustration bit through her. Why did he have to be so stubborn? "I'm not going to let you do this."

He just shook his head, his eyes full of resolve. "And I'm not going to let you throw your life away, Cecile."

"You don't get to make that decision for me."

He leaned against his desk, his head down. Silence hung in the air between them as each waited for the other to give in. She wasn't giving up on this relationship as easily as he seemed to be able to do.

He sighed and straightened, then looked at her. Suddenly, the distance between had grown into an uncrossable canyon.

His face was hard and cold as he removed his hat and faced her. "I can't deny I have feelings for you, Cecile, but we've both been fooling ourselves if we think this thing between us could ever work. It would be too hard, and I don't want you enough to put in that much effort."

She sucked in a breath as his words hit her like a gut punch. Tears welled in her eyes and she nearly lost her footing.

She was certain he was only saying those terrible things in order to push her away but she was still so insecure about being wanted. It was all too easy to believe that his feelings for her were less than hers—that it was easy for him to let her go. That she wasn't good enough.

Pain stole her breath but she had to say something. Anger roared through her and all she could think to do was lash out at him. "If you think I can keep working for you after this then you're crazy. I have offers, Josh. A lot of offers."

He nodded but his expression didn't waver. "I know. You should accept one of them. It's time you moved on from Courtland County."

The color drained from Cecile's face at his words and he could see she was struggling to keep from crying. Finally, she turned and marched out of his office.

He fell into his chair as sorrow washed through him. That had been brutal but necessary. She would never have let go of her life here without that terrible lie coming from his mouth.

It was the best thing for her and he had to focus on what she needed. That was all that mattered to him.

Her anger and pride would force her hand. She would take one of those job offers and leave Courtland, and him, in the rearview mirror.

It wasn't what he wanted, but it was what had to be.

God, forgive me.

Cecile felt everyone's eyes on her as she worked at her desk. They knew something was wrong but didn't know what had happened between her and Josh. Or maybe they did. Their sheriff's office was tiny, and the walls weren't all that thick. For all she knew, they'd heard every word that transpired between them.

She choked back tears as she finished typing up her resignation letter then printed it off. She retrieved it from the printer, signed it, then marched into Josh's office and plopped it down in front of him. "This is my letter of resignation effective immediately. I'll work out my two weeks' notice if you need me to."

He waved that idea away, just as she had expected him to. On that point, she was sure his thinking aligned with hers. Two weeks of awkward passes in the office? No, thank you. "It's not necessary but thanks." He stared up at her. She saw regret in his face and hoped he would change his mind, sweep her up into his arms, tell her it had all been a horrible mistake and do his best to kiss away the hurt and anger she was struggling to keep contained.

He did none of those things.

"Fine. I'll clean out my desk today and update the task force team on the status of the investigation."

He nodded. "Where did you decide to go?"

"Lakeland County. I'm meeting with the sheriff tomorrow."

"They have a good force. You'll be an asset to their team over there."

Indignation flooded her. That was all he had to say to her after all the years they'd worked together? She stiffened and jutted her chin into the air then placed her service weapon and badge on his desk. "Goodbye, Josh." She turned and walked out of his office and into the conference room to brief the task force and say her goodbyes.

It was difficult telling the team that she was leaving. It was even harder leaving the task force knowing the case remained unsolved. Lakeland County hadn't experienced any murders that fit the criteria and thus wasn't included in the task force. She felt like she was abandoning Erica and the other victims as she packed up her desk, said her goodbyes to her coworkers and walked out to her rental car, but she couldn't spend another day working in that office with Josh. Her heart would never be able to take it.

She headed out of town, fighting back tears. She wanted nothing more than to go home, curl up on the couch and have a good cry, but if she did that she might change her mind. She had to keep moving or she would fall completely apart.

She stopped by her father's, spilling everything that had happened to him over a cup of coffee. She hadn't meant to tell him so much but she couldn't leave town without letting him know why.

He reached across the table and took her hand. "You have to do what's right for you, CeCe. You deserve better."

She didn't know what she'd expected from him—he wasn't a man to show his feelings—but sympathy hadn't been it. That did it for her. She burst into tears and, surprisingly, her father hugged her until her tears were spent.

Her entire life had been spent right here in Courtland and mostly on this ranch. It had been a good life, too. Her father wasn't overly sentimental but he'd taken good care of her.

She wiped away tears. "I texted Andy. I'm going to stay with him until I find an apartment and a place to stable Sunflower." Her brother and his wife had a vacant apartment over their garage and had quickly offered it to her for as long as she needed it when she'd asked. But she wanted a place of her own, a place that wouldn't remind her of all she didn't have—a spouse and kids…a family. Staying there too long would only serve to rub salt into her already open wound.

"What about this guy that's after you? Aren't you still in danger?"

She'd turned in her service weapon to Josh before she'd left, but she still had a backup. Besides, once she was out of town and no longer investigating this case, she felt certain she would be safe enough. "Once I'm in Lakeland, I should be fine. There haven't been any murders there that fit the profile. It's obviously out of his comfort zone. I'll be extra careful though just in case."

Her father hugged her one last time, made her promise to call him when she got settled, then watched her as she pulled away. She was leaving her childhood home behind along with a job and town she loved. It broke her heart…but it was nothing compared to how her heart was breaking over Josh Avery.

She drove home and washed her face, doing her best not to stare at her reflection in the mirror. She couldn't believe she'd cried in front of her father or his reaction. Funny, it seemed they were finally connecting now that she was leaving.

How ironic.

She pressed a towel to her face, noticing the puffiness around her eyes already settling in. She had to move on. She couldn't dwell on it. She'd lost Josh. She'd lost the future she'd dreamed of. There was nothing left for her in Courtland County.

Her phone rang. She picked it up and checked the caller ID.

Josh. No doubt calling to try to explain. To try to ask her for…something. She didn't know what. He would probably say that he didn't want to lose her friendship, yet he wasn't willing to take the next step to salvage their relationship.

She tossed down the phone. She couldn't deal with his guilt. If he didn't want her, then it was time to move on. She picked up the information she'd printed out for an apartment complex in Lakeland. She'd emailed Sheriff Jefferson earlier and scheduled an appointment to see him tomorrow. They had a good investigation team and he'd expressed an interest in having her join it several times. Lakeland was far enough to feel like a fresh start. Leaving Courtland behind was breaking her heart, but it was a necessary step. It was time she stopped pining over someone she could never have.

She was good at her job and she enjoyed it. That would have to be enough. Finding justice for those who'd been wronged. In her job she saw all kinds of terrible things, the depths of evil that men could stoop to. She had no business whining and crying over a lack of love in her life, not after what she'd seen.

She walked into her bedroom and pulled down her suitcase. Packing it seemed like giving up, but it was what she had to do.

She finished packing and set her suitcase by the bed to grab when she left tomorrow morning. A noise outside grabbed her attention. She peered out the window but didn't see anything out of the ordinary. She reached for her spare gun and walked through the house. Her father's concerns about her safety were valid. She had been the killer's target. He'd even attacked her right here in her own house already. She meant what she'd told her father. Lakeland was far enough away that she didn't believe she would be in danger any longer. But she wasn't gone yet.

She checked the windows, wondering if she was going crazy. She was hearing things but she justified it as she was rattled by this breakup with Josh. Could she even call it a breakup when there had barely even been a relationship?

She walked into the kitchen, set down her gun and filled a pan to boil pasta. This might be the last meal she made in this house. Tomorrow would be the start of a new day for her, a new life.

She took out a bell pepper and tomato to add to her salad, grabbed a knife and cut them up. She set it down and moved to the stove to stir the pasta. Her brain was already ticking off things she needed to take care of as she poured spaghetti sauce into a pan then put garlic toast into the oven to brown. There were cases she cared about seeing solved, most importantly Erica's case. She trusted everyone at the office to put their best efforts into finding the killer, but she wouldn't just walk away from it. She might be hand-ing it off officially but that didn't mean she would ever stop investigating it, not until Erica's killer was brought to justice.

Suddenly, a knock at the door grabbed her attention.

She glanced at the clock. She wasn't expecting anyone. She walked to the door and peered through the peephole. Tom Rainer—her old classmate who worked at the Henderson Ranch.

She opened the door. "Tom, hi."

"Hi, Cecile. I heard through the rumor mill that you were leaving town soon. I know it's late but I'm one of the volunteers for the food and clothing pantry, and I was hoping I could get that donation of clothes before you left. We're hosting the pantry this weekend."

She'd forgotten all about her promise. Good thing he'd come by tonight. If he'd waited another day, she would have been gone. "Of course. I'm sorry I haven't gotten it to you before now. Life has been chaotic." She'd meant to drop it by with Mrs. Avery but she hadn't even been home to get it since the anniversary party. She pushed open the door and invited him inside.

"I understand. Tracking down a killer is a big job—especially a serial killer. Everyone in town is on edge. I know several of the women at church who refuse to go out at night alone anymore."

"Well, that's good advice at any time. Let me grab that box for you." She walked into the hallway and opened the closet where she'd stowed the box of clothes she'd put aside for the drive.

"How's the investigation going? Are you making any progress?"

She was used to the questions. People were frightened and they had every right to be—and they were also curious. It was just human nature. "We'll find him. Don't worry." She carried the box into the living room and handed it to him.

He took it from her. "You seem very confident that you're going to catch this guy."

"I am. He's getting sloppy and he's going to make a mistake. When he does, that will be his undoing."

"Do you really believe you can catch him?"

"I know I can." She could…if she were staying in town. Someone else would have to catch him now.

He smiled, then glanced toward the kitchen and sniffed. "Is something burning?"

"Oh, I forgot." She hurried into the kitchen

and removed a tray of garlic toast from the oven, letting out a frustrated sigh when she saw it was black and burned. She set the pan on the stove to cool. She hadn't been expecting company and had forgotten all about it. Now she would need to make another batch.

It was time for Tom to go. She started to tell him so but as she turned, Tom slammed something over her head, sending her to the floor. The room spun and pain encircled her but when she tried to reach for something to defend herself, she only managed to knock over the pan of spaghetti sauce.

He grabbed a handful of her hair and yanked as he hovered over her. "I've got you now." His voice was low and menacing. She recognized it as that of the man who'd attacked her at the hospital, then phoned her at the station. She realized her mistake too late. She'd profiled that this serial was capable of blending in and seeming nonthreatening, and Tom certainly had presented as such. She'd let her guard down around him just as the other women he'd murdered had done.

Panic rose inside her. She couldn't let him take her. She had to figure out a way to get free from him. She flailed her legs and kicked over the island, sending pans crashing to the floor. Tom cursed and pinned her to the floor. She scratched and kicked at him but he easily overpowered her, pressing his hands into her neck in a choke hold.

Her vision began to fade. She was losing consciousness fast, and if that happened, she was doomed. She'd seen the images of his victims. She wouldn't survive if she couldn't fight back.

She'd fought him off before, but she had no leverage against him flat on her back. He'd obviously come better prepared than last time. He was too forceful and her strength began to wane as he bore down on her.

Her arms fell to her side and all the fight flowed from her as things began to dim.

This was it. This was how it ended for her.

She was going to die.

NINE

Josh did his best to concentrate on paperwork but he was restless, unable to sit still all afternoon. And each time he glanced at the bullpen and saw the empty desk Cecile once occupied, his heart broke all over again.

Finally, after several hours, he pushed to his feet and put the paperwork aside. He couldn't concentrate and pretending otherwise wasn't going to do any good.

He wandered into the conference room where Zeke and Greg were still working the case. They had little to update. Cecile had trained them well but no one could ever really train someone to have her sense of focus and attention to details. How were they ever going to solve this case without her?

He spotted his brother Paul entering the office. "I've got some news about Frank Henderson," Paul announced.

Josh led him into his office and shut the door. "What did you find?"

"I have a friend who works for the ATF. Apparently, they're investigating Henderson for possible gun running."

"That explains the need for the increased security—and the fact that he needs all that land without any animals on it."

"It sure does. They believe he's flying guns in and storing them underground. That lake it looked like they were building on his property was more than likely going to conceal a bunker to store weapons."

"No wonder he's so insistent on people not trespassing. He didn't want anyone to find out about his side business."

"Exactly. My friend says they've had an agent working undercover in Henderson's operation ever since a former girlfriend of Frank's nephew, Bryce, approached them with the information. The ATF is planning a raid on his property soon."

That explained a lot about Henderson's behavior. Josh was glad for the information. "Do we know who the undercover agent is?"

Paul nodded. "You met him."

"Kennedy?" Henderson's head of security was an ATF agent? That was wild. "Thanks for the information." At least he knew Henderson and Kennedy were probably not involved in the murders they were investigating. Each of them had their own reasons to stay off the radar of the local police.

Josh left the office and climbed into his pickup. He placed his hat on the seat beside him and shifted the truck into gear. He was already on the highway heading toward Cecile's house to tell her the news before he realized where he was going. He couldn't explain his need to see her again but it was strong.

He slammed on the brakes, sending the truck to the side of the road. He slammed his fist against the steering wheel. He couldn't keep doing this. He was only making it worse for them both. He'd been the one to tell her to leave, but then he'd found an excuse to call her earlier. She'd let his calls go to voicemail, proof that she didn't want to talk to him. Now he was heading to her house? He couldn't continue to hold on to her.

His radio buzzed and he was glad to have something else to occupy his mind. "Avery. What's up?"

Marla's voice spoke back to him. "Sheriff, we just received a call from a neighbor of Cecile's. He was walking by and saw some suspicious activity at her house. We've tried calling her on her cell phone and she's not picking up. I'm sending a car to check it out. Wanted to let you know."

"I'm closer. I'll check it out myself."

She was still a target, so why had he let her go alone? Neither of them had been thinking rationally. He'd been so busy protecting her from him that they'd forgotten about a killer on the loose. And what situation was she facing now, all on her own? He had a hunch that it was serious. Cecile's neighbors were spread out and very private. Not the kind to call in over nothing.

He pushed the truck back into Drive and headed toward her house.

Her rental car was still there when he arrived. That meant she was home. On the drive over, he'd tried calling her but it had just rung out to voice mail. He could understand her ignoring his calls, but surely she wouldn't ignore Zeke's or Greg's or Marla's. He knew they were trying to reach her, too, and that they'd have called him if they'd been able to talk to her. But why would they not have been able to get her to answer? Even if she was mad at him, even if she was leaving Courtland County and the sheriff's office behind, she was still their friend. She wouldn't leave them hanging out to dry like that. It wasn't her way.

He got out and walked to the door, expecting her front door to open and her to demand to know what he was doing there. But it didn't open. He knocked but heard no sounds coming from inside. That was odd. He walked around the house but saw nothing out of the ordinary. He tried her phone again and heard it ringing from inside.

He drew his weapon as a bad feeling rushed through him. He hurried to a window, the bile in his gut rising with each step. He peered inside and his heart fell. He could see clear evidence of a struggle in the kitchen.

He kicked in the back door, stepped inside and glanced around. The island was overturned and things had been pushed off the cabinets. Spaghetti noodles and sauce covered the floor.

He got on his radio and called dispatch. "Send a team to Cecile's house. Something's wrong here. It looks like she was attacked." He hurried down the hall calling her name.

The house was empty.

No, no, no.

He holstered his gun and tried to figure out

what had happened here as sirens screamed in the distance. There'd been no evidence of a break-in, which meant she'd let the assailant inside.

She'd turned her back on him. She'd fought back but she'd lost and he'd taken her. He didn't even have to wonder who the attacker was. He didn't know the man's name or identity but he knew it was the same man they'd been tracking. He'd entered and taken Cecile, just as he'd been trying to for days now.

She was gone.

It didn't take long for his team to jump into gear and secure the house as a crime scene.

Zeke approached him. "Sheriff, Forensics is taking fingerprints and collecting evidence."

"Have they found any blood?"

"It doesn't look like it. It looks like she was cooking when he attacked. Her gun was lying on the counter and there was a cutting knife on the floor by the island."

She'd been startled. She hadn't seen it coming. He stared at the half-packed suitcase on her bed and realized she'd been focused on getting ready to leave. That was probably why he'd been able to surprise her. He touched a wet spot on her suitcase. Tears. Had she been crying? He suspected she had been. He saw evidence of tissue in the trash and a wet cloth in the bathroom. He kicked himself. It hurt him to know he'd caused those tears.

He'd pushed her away, however, now that she was gone, all he could think was how much he wanted her back. Fear paralyzed him at the thought that she might already be dead. He shook that thought away. He couldn't go there. He had to operate on the assumption that she was still alive until they knew differently.

He turned to Zeke, who was waiting for him to respond. "Put out a BOLO for her. Set up roadblocks in the area. No one gets out until we find her."

"What exactly are we looking for, Josh?"

He didn't have the answer to that. "I don't know yet. For now, focus on anything out of the ordinary."

As awareness returned to her, Cecile realized she was lying on her stomach on a concrete floor. The events prior to her losing consciousness rushed back and she sat up quickly. Her hands were tied behind her back, her legs were bound with duct tape and her throat was burning.

She couldn't tell where she was but it was dark and stank of oil and gasoline.

She turned over and looked up. She was at the bottom of an automotive bay in a garage. That explained the gas and oil smells. Seated in a chair at the top of the ledge and staring down at her was her assailant. He smiled broadly and her blood boiled.

"Tom Rainer. Let me go." She pulled at her binds as anger surged through her, but they were tight. He'd had plenty of practice at this. She wasn't going to be able to escape them easily.

"I can't do that, Cecile."

"What do you want with me? Why did you bring me here?"

"Do you recognize this place? It belonged to my grandfather. I used to play here as a child. It's been closed down for years but my family still owns it, giving us the perfect spot to spend a little time together."

The tone in his voice was cold. She should have known it was Rainer all along. He fit all of the profile criteria. He'd been at the party and had been inserting himself into her life for the past few weeks. She'd been so busy looking for the killer that she hadn't seen him standing right in front of her. Now the oil and gasoline drops they'd found on several of the victims made sense, too.

She'd suspected it would be someone she knew but couldn't have imagined Tom Rainer had the capability to brutally murder multiple women. She'd known him since they were kids. And Erica had never been anything but nice to him. "You did this, Tom? You killed all those women? You killed Erica? Why?"

Tom smiled, actually looking a little nostalgic. "Erica was special to me. She was my first. I went to that party that night not looking to hurt anyone. I only knew I was restless. When I saw Erica go off by herself, I followed her. I couldn't help myself. I couldn't stop watching her. I couldn't pull myself away."

Cecile closed her eyes. She didn't want to hear this. He might have felt that he had been compelled to kill Erica, but his subsequent murders had been well thought out and carefully planned. His compulsions had turned to enjoyment.

"She was my first." His smile was twisted and chilling. "But you won't be my last."

Her heart hammered and her mouth went dry. He was only confessing to her now because he didn't plan on her ever being able to tell anyone. She was going to die here at the hands of this man.

"You murdered twelve women."

He smiled again. "Those are just the ones you know of. The real number is actually larger than that."

They'd only looked at cases where the bodies had been found and no one had been convicted for the crime. If he was being honest, they would need to look at missing persons' cases, too, and possibly some cases where an innocent person might have been accused.

Not you—you won't be looking into anything. The task force will have to handle it without you. You'll be dead and they won't even know to look.

"How many?" she demanded. "I'm going to die anyway, so you may as well tell me."

He thought for a moment, then nodded. "Most of the ones you don't know about were when I was living away from Courtland but there was one here. Someone I think you know of. A murder for which someone very special to you was accused."

Josh! He was talking about Haley's murder, flaunting it in her face. But she wasn't that gullible. It didn't match his other cases, which meant he was probably making up this confession just to taunt her. "Nothing about that case connects it to the other murders."

"You don't believe me?"

She glared at him and shook her head. He was only trying to get a rise out of her and she wasn't going to give him that satisfaction.

He knelt a few feet away from her, his eyes glaring into hers. "It was different because I got interrupted. Your boyfriend came home early and the woman fought me. She shoved away from me but then she lost her balance and smashed her head against the island. I never even got a chance to tie her up, much less do anything else." He sounded disappointed.

Cecile sucked in a deep breath. He'd just described how Haley had died. He really had been there! Josh could finally be exonerated!

Only she would never be able to tell him so. It was a confession that would go to the grave with her. No one was coming to look for her. Josh and the other deputies would assume she'd left town. By the next morning, people might realize she was gone—but it would be far too late by then. She glanced at Rainer and realized he knew the same thing.

"You're all alone, Cecile. No one is coming for you."

But someone knew where she was. Someone knew she was in danger. God. No matter what, God was still there with her. He was still watching out for her. He might not intervene—He didn't always or else she wouldn't have a job—but she knew in her heart that He was here watching her, comforting her, and would welcome her when she left this life.

Only she wasn't ready to die. She wasn't ready to leave Josh. She loved him even if he wasn't willing to admit he loved her, too. She should have waited for him to get past his fears. She shouldn't have issued him that ultimatum of accepting another job. What had she been thinking?

"What happened to you, Tom? You used to be a decent person. What happened that distorted your personality so completely?"

He jumped up and flung the chair across the room, sending it clanging against the wall as he walked down the steps toward her. She flinched as he approached her. "What's wrong with me? There is *nothing* wrong with me," he shouted at her. "The problem is you and people like you. You're twisted and cruel and like to try to torture men with your eyes and your body. You're the sick ones. I'm just taking back what you tried to steal from me."

She sucked in a breath at his outburst. Power. That was what he wanted. His mind was so corrupted and warped that there would be no talking him out of his ritual. He'd been killing for years and had his routine down. She'd interrupted that and caused his anger to focus on her. Years of practice and a murderous rage were all now aimed squarely at her.

This was what he'd done to his victims. He'd watched them, observed them, looking and waiting for an excuse that fueled his anger and rage. Then he would capture them and direct all his fury at them until he snuffed out their lives and disposed of their bodies. Then the cycle would begin again.

He grabbed her and stuffed a rag into her mouth before marching back up the stairs. He pulled the portable stairs up so that even if she managed to get loose, she wouldn't be able to go anywhere. She listened to him walk out, the sound of the garage doors slamming shut and signaling her doom. The lights flickered off and everything went dark. She was alone, but she knew that she didn't have long before he returned and finished what he'd started. He had the perfect place to house his victims long enough to torture and kill them.

She wrinkled her nose as she breathed in the

stench of the pit she was in. It stank of something other than oil and gas. It was the odor of bodies being trapped here for days before being slaughtered. He might have tried to clean up after himself, but some things couldn't be fully washed away. They always lingered.

A wave of sorrow filled her and a tear slipped down her cheek. She wasn't going to escape this place. She knew what was in store for her. She'd seen the evidence of it on the other women's bodies in the photographs that she'd studied. She knew what was coming for her. And what was coming for Josh when someone found her body dumped on the side of the road.

She closed her eyes and tried to stop the image of how his life would be affected by it. He would blame himself. Of course, he would. He would blame himself for pushing her away. She didn't want him to suffer that but Tom would make certain he did. He wouldn't hide her. He would want the maximum exposure of his work and the maximum damage to those she cared about.

He'd perfected his process over the years, spending more time with his victims and torturing them. And now she was going to see his process firsthand.

She allowed the tears and sobs to flow as she realized this was the end for her.

God, please help me.

Josh paced the conference room. He was surrounded by the evidence that had to lead him to Cecile's whereabouts yet he had no idea how to find her. She hadn't been able to crack this mass of information. How was he expected to do it now that her life was on the line?

He had Zeke, Greg, Marla and the rest of the task force digging back through everything and he'd even enlisted his brothers' help along with Brooke, who used to be an army investigator. He'd also brought in his dad. He needed all eyes on this information. Anyone who wanted to help, he was willing to let them try. He would do whatever it took to find Cecile.

But it had been hours and he wasn't even certain she was still alive. His worst fear was receiving a phone call about finding her body dumped on the side of the road.

No, he couldn't allow himself to give in to despair. She was alive until he heard otherwise. This guy might have been on a killing spree but he'd become obsessed with Cecile.

He would take his time with her. That gave them some leeway in finding her, but not much.

He glanced at the images of the women they'd found and knew that even though the murderer might not kill her right away, she was still in danger.

Marla stuck her head into the conference room. "Sheriff, Mr. Richardson is here."

He thanked her and hurried out to meet Cecile's dad. Josh had sent a deputy to bring him to the office. Another last-ditch effort to uncover any clue that might help him find her.

He stuck out his hand. "Thank you for coming, sir."

Mr. Richardson shook his hand and took a seat on a bench. Josh pulled up a chair and sat opposite him.

"What's going on? Your deputy said something had happened to my CeCe? I thought she was in Lakeland looking at apartments."

"She never made it. I went by her house and found evidence of a struggle—and no sign of Cecile. We believe the man we've been searching for got to her and abducted her from her house."

He tapped his hand against his knee in a thoughtful gesture. He was a man of few emotions but Josh saw the worry around his mouth and eyes.

"I'm going to do everything in my power to find her and bring her home," Josh assured him.

He pinned Josh with a hard stare. "She thinks a lot of you. It broke her heart to make the decision to leave here."

Josh lowered his face in shame but nodded and clutched his hands together. "I know. That was a mistake. It should never have happened. I don't want her to leave, sir."

"You care for my daughter?"

Josh looked at him and nodded. He hadn't admitted it to another person but now he felt compelled to do so. "Very much."

Earl Richardson locked eyes with him. "Don't let her down, Josh."

"I'll do my best." He stood. "I'll have my deputy drive you back home."

"No, I'll stick around here for a while if that's all right. I want to be close by for any updates."

Josh nodded his agreement, then arranged for someone to bring Earl a cup of coffee before he headed back into the conference room.

"Please tell me you've found something," he pleaded with the room at large.

No one spoke up and several even lowered their heads, looking ashamed.

Zeke pushed a hand through his hair. "Let's face it, Josh. If Cecile couldn't figure this out, what chance do we have?"

Zeke was on the verge of giving up. He saw it on the younger man's face and on some of the others', too. They didn't know how to solve this.

Brooke stood. "Let's go back through the list Cecile prepared of the people who were at the party. If we go through them one by one, maybe we'll find something."

"That's going to take forever," Colby told her.

They both looked to Josh. "Do it," he told them. "Until we have another direction, we have to do what we can do." Work the problem from any angle they could find. That was what Cecile would do. He just prayed that once they found something, it wouldn't be too late for her. He checked his watch. She'd been missing for six hours. How long would this unknown assailant keep Cecile alive?

God, please keep her safe and guide our paths.

The conference room door opened and Marla rushed in holding a group of photos.

"I found these on Cecile's printer. She must not have had an opportunity to follow up on them."

He scanned through the images, recognizing several people from her list of men who'd been at the party. "Any idea why she singled these men out?"

Marla shook her head. "She didn't mention anything to me about them."

The others shook their heads too. Whatever lead Cecile had been following up on, she hadn't had the opportunity to share with the others.

"Pin these up on the board. Let's focus on these first. I trust Cecile's instincts. If she found a lead, we need to finish it."

It didn't take long for them to figure out that all the men in the photographs Cecile had printed out had military backgrounds but, an hour later, they were still at it, looking for something, anything, that might clue them into the killer's identity.

"I know him."

Josh and everyone else in the room turned to see Earl Richardson standing and staring at the wall of images of people they were discussing. How had he entered the room without anyone noticing?

Josh slid off his perch on the edge of the table and zeroed in on the photograph Earl was referring to. It showed Tom Rainer, a member of Henderson's security team and an old classmate of Cecile's.

"He used to do odd jobs for me at the farm back when he was a teenager. He used to follow my CeCe around like a lovesick puppy."

That caught Josh's attention. "Cecile never mentioned they had any kind of relationship."

"I don't think she ever even noticed him. He didn't work for me long. I caught him hurting some of the animals. Fired him on the spot. After that, his family moved to Leake County and he transferred schools. I was glad of it. I didn't want my kids around him. He was one oddball. I heard through the grapevine he had trouble all the way through school. His parents were mighty disappointed. They were good people and couldn't imagine how they ended up with such a troublemaker. His grandparents took him in after his parents died in a car crash."

Josh's father stood. "I remember that. Their car went off the road and rammed a tree. The son was in the back seat and was the only one who survived. His family owned that old service station over off the highway, didn't they?"

Earl nodded. "They sure did. Always hoped Tom would take over the business, too, but from what I understand, he never had any interest in it. They were forced to close it down when the grandfather got sick several years ago."

The mention of the service station sparked something in Josh. He turned and looked at the list of similarities that Cecile had noted between the victims. Several of them had had traces of used motor oil and grease on their bodies, clothes and hair. An abandoned service station would give Rainer a place to hold victims without anyone interrupting him and could also account for the traces of motor oil and grease.

He glanced at the sketch the two women from his folks' anniversary party had given them. It looked similar enough to Tom Rainer.

"Brooke, pull up a background check on Rainer."

She typed his name into the computer search system. "He didn't graduate from high school but took and passed his GED when he was seventeen. He joined the army but was discharged after only one year for disorderly conduct. He had a string of suspected assaults against women but no convictions."

Zeke joined in the conversation. "And he works security at the Henderson Ranch so he would know how to time moving Erica's body without getting caught."

Rainer was checking off a lot of boxes. "And he was definitely at the party the night Erica died. It's the best lead we have." It wasn't a smoking gun but at least it was a direction for them to investigate. "Brooke, find out everything else you can on Tom Rainer. I want to know everything there is to know about him. And I want to get eyes on that service station." He headed for the door.

Colby stood. "I'm coming with you."

"Me, too," Paul stated and Miles and Lawson also offered to help, along with Zeke, Greg and Chet.

He was glad to know he had so many people on his side to help. He would need them all if he wanted to bring Cecile back alive. "Let's go, then."

He grabbed his gear and climbed into his brother's SUV as Paul climbed in beside him.

"She'll be okay," Paul assured him. "We'll find her and bring her home."

Josh prayed he was right and that it wasn't too late.

She'd been in the dark for what seemed like hours when tires crunching on the gravel outside the building alerted her that someone was coming. Her pulse kicked up a notch. Tom was back to finish her off. Her time had run out.

The garage doors opened and moments later the lights flickered back on. A shadow played on the wall, growing larger as the figure approached, until Tom appeared at the top of the bay. He lowered the stairs and climbed down.

Cecile scrambled to push herself away but it did little good.

He laughed at her feeble attempt. "There's no escape, Cecile." He pulled a knife from his coat pocket and stepped closer. "You and I are going to take our time and have some fun."

Hope faltered inside her for a moment but she'd decided she wasn't going down without a fight. He was going to have to get close to her if he wanted to either use that knife or planned to strangle her and she was going to make him regret it when he did.

She pressed herself against the bay wall and held her breath. She wanted to fight him the moment he approached but she needed to wait for the best opening. Needed to let him get closer. The moment he did, she struck, kicking him hard in the knee. He screamed and went down but jumped up and reached for her.

"You little—"

She headbutted him. Hard.

He cried out again and stumbled backward.

Pain bristled through Cecile but she did her best to keep her senses about her while he went down. She scrambled to grab the knife, cut her hands and feet loose then pulled out the rag and pushed to her feet, running toward the stairs. She was nearly to the top when he grabbed her ankle. She kicked him again, this time in the face, sending him reeling backward again, screaming and cursing at her.

Cecile reached the top, then took off running. The first door she tried was locked. She wasn't getting out that way. She turned and sprinted through the mostly empty building looking for an escape while Tom's footfalls indicated he was coming after her.

"You won't get away, Cecile," he hollered at her.

She found a sliding door and managed to pull it open a few inches before it caught. The echo of his voice told her Tom was getting closer. She had to get out of this building if she had any hope of surviving. She pushed through the narrow opening, barely managing to scrape her way through.

No other buildings were in sight but a wooded area backed up to the building. She could try to sneak around the front of the building and hotwire his car to drive away, but she suspected she didn't have that kind of time before he found her. He knew the building and the surroundings far better than she did—he wouldn't have to search for an exit. Her only choice was to take cover in the woods and pray she would come out on the other side somewhere she could call for help.

She darted into the woods as Tom screamed out her name again.

TEN

Josh pulled on his bulletproof vest as his team prepared to surround the old service station. He was certain Tom Rainer was holed up there and this was the place where he'd taken Cecile and the other women. He checked his weapon, then sent up a prayer for Cecile's safety. They needed to get to her as soon as possible. He couldn't even let himself question whether or not she was still alive. She had to be. He couldn't go on if she wasn't.

He motioned for his brothers to take the back of the station and Colby and Paul and Miles all headed off with their respective teams. He wasn't alone. He had to remember that. He had God and he had his family with him. He could get through this.

He waited until his brothers each checked in that they'd taken their positions, before he turned to Zeke. He reminded his brother-in-law about the plan they'd formulated on the drive. Zeke was going to remain outside with other deputies and set up the lights on his command while also flanking the area to make certain Rainer didn't slip past them.

Josh took a deep breath and ran to the front. At his command, they all breached the facility at the same time. The lights from outside flickered on, illuminating the abandoned service station but there still remained shadowed areas where Rainer could be hiding.

Josh moved toward the center of the building. He heard his brothers each checking in and proclaiming the place clear of occupants. He aimed his gun ahead of him and moved toward them. His breath was heavy and his heart hammered. He did his best to listen to the sounds of the area. If Cecile were here, she would find a way to alert him.

He pushed through but when he spotted Miles, he relaxed his stance a bit. They were all converging in the same spot. That meant they'd been through the building and found no signs of anyone.

"This place is clear," Miles stated. "They're not here."

"Anywhere else he could have gone?" Paul asked.

Josh shook his head. "This was the place owned by his grandfather. It's the only place he'd have easy access to that fits the descriptions. If he didn't bring his victims here, he must have somewhere off the grid where he keeps them."

He put away his gun and gave a heavy sigh. He'd been so certain they would be here. The motor oil evidence had seemed solid.

God, where is she?

He walked through the building. He remembered when this was a working station and his father used to bring his cars here to be serviced by old man Rainer. It had been closed for years. Just another family-owned business that hadn't had to close.

If only Cecile were here to help him think through this. He nearly laughed at that thought. He needed Cecile to help him find Cecile. It was a never-ending circle that only proved to him how essential she was to his life. Not just professionally, either. He was lost without her.

"Sheriff, we found evidence of blood."

Josh hurried into the garage area to find Zeke down in the auto bay. He walked to the bottom to see where Zeke pointed. He bent down and stared at it, then touched it. It was still wet. "It's fresh. Someone was here recently and it seems like a possible struggle occurred."

Colby nodded at him. "Cecile would have fought back if she was able."

He knew that was right. He stood and surveyed the area. The sliding glass doors stood open, leading to woods behind the station. "If she managed to get away from him, she would have run into the woods where she could hide."

Paul nodded. "I agree. I'll put together a team to start searching."

Colby took out his phone. "I'm going to call around and try to find a helicopter we can use. It'll make the search easier."

Josh stared out at the vast wilderness before him. It was several acres of uncut land with lots of places to hide.

His instinct was to dart off after her but he waited on his brother. As sheriff, Josh had had to coordinate searches through woods like this before and knew it wasn't easy to find someone, especially when that someone was trying to hide from an attacker. And Rainer would be triggered once he realized they were looking for him and might lash out and kill her.

Josh and his brothers each took an armed team in a different direction. If Cecile and Rainer were out here, they would find them. He just prayed it wouldn't be too late.

Cecile was a fighter. Rainer was used to targeting women who weren't trained. If the blood on the floor of the garage indicated anything, it was that Cecile had fought back. He just needed her to keep fighting, keep surviving, until he could find her.

Lord, please guide our steps and keep her safe until I can reach her.

Cecile darted through the woods, pushing away the limbs and brush that scratched her arms and face. She couldn't slow down. Rainer was out here tracking her. Maybe running into the woods hadn't been the best idea but at least she had some cover. Rainer had been military and was probably trained in survival tactics, but Cecile had had four brothers. She'd been left in the woods numerous times to fend for herself and she'd learned to do so. She had to keep going and not quit until she could find a way to reach Josh.

Despite her determination, she finally had to stop to catch her breath. She did her best to orient herself based on the position of the sun. She was heading north, which meant she should hit the main highway by Henderson Ranch before long, if she wasn't turned around. They would have a phone she could use to call Josh.

She pushed through a brush of limbs and into a clearing overlooking a cliff. The highway was nowhere in sight. And there was no way to get to it even if she could see it. She had gotten herself turned around. Maybe she wasn't as adept at navigation as she'd thought. Wherever she was, she had to find her way out.

Rustling in the trees caused her heart to race. She spun around. There was nowhere to run. The only escape was down the cliff and she would never survive that.

Movement in the trees.

She was trapped.

A figure pushed through the brush, visible at first only by the barrel of the gun.

A smile broke Tom's face as he spotted her. "I wanted a challenge and you sure showed me one. But, in the end, I win, Cecile. I always win."

Running was fruitless. He would shoot her before she could even get to cover. But she couldn't just stand here and let him kill her, either. The one advantage she had was that she knew he didn't want to shoot her. He wanted to kill her with his bare hands, up close and personal. That was how he got his satisfaction. If she couldn't stop him from killing her, at least she could rob him of the satisfaction of enjoying it.

Only, she wasn't ready to die.

"Get on the ground," he commanded her, moving closer to where she stood.

She hedged her options, still hoping, still praying, for some way out of this.

"I said get on the ground," he shouted.

She fell to her knees and he approached her, reaching into his pocket and pulling out a plastic zip tie. Her chances for escaping her binds twice were practically zero. If he managed to tie her up again, she was going to die.

But she still had his knife. She gripped her hand around it and when he crouched down to bind her hands, she swiped it at him, feeling the blade dig into his flesh. Then she sprang to her feet and took off running. That cut wasn't enough to stop him but if she could reach the tree line, she could hide again.

He swore and fired the gun. Something stung her leg and sent her tumbling. Her hands broke her fall but she spun around to see blood pool on her jeans as pain ripped through her.

He'd shot her.

He tossed the gun and pinned her to the ground, using his body weight to keep her still. He grabbed her hands and wasted no time in pinning them to the ground. She struggled against him but he had the optimal position.

He grabbed her neck and choked her as her vision began to fade.

Josh turned and headed toward the sound of gunfire. Colby was beside him and let him know their brothers had heard it, too, and were on the way.

His heart was in his throat as he burst through the clearing and spotted Cecile on the ground with Rainer on top of her. He was choking her.

Josh lifted his gun and took aim. "Get off her!"

Rainer dove for his weapon, grabbed Cecile and pulled her up in front of him to use her as a shield, all in one quick motion.

Time slowed as Rainer contemplated his options. He was cornered but still dangerous. "Let her go," Josh repeated.

Instead of giving up, Rainer pressed the gun against Cecile's head. Her face paled and Josh could see the fear in her eyes.

For a moment, Josh couldn't move. The thought of losing Cecile, of living without her, had him paralyzed. He couldn't do this alone.

Then, he remembered. He wasn't alone. His brothers were beside him and understood what was at risk. And God. He had God.

"Let's just settle down," Colby spoke calmly to Rainer, doing his best to defuse the situation.

"Everything is going to be okay," Josh stated. He pulled his eyes off Cecile and locked stares with Rainer. "Let her go."

"Get back!" Rainer pressed the gun even more tightly against her head. He was losing control. He was caught and he knew it. He'd already killed multiple women. He had nothing to lose by killing Cecile. He saw it in Rainer's face. He wasn't interested in notoriety or a lengthy trial. He wanted to go out in a blaze of glory.

That didn't bode well for Cecile.

Rainer turned his gun toward them. Josh fired as did his brothers. Rainer went down but not before shoving Cecile. She stumbled and lost her balance near the edge of the cliff and Josh's heart jumped to his throat as she disappeared over the edge.

"No!" Josh screamed as he dropped his gun and ran to the cliff's edge.

Cecile stared up at him, her hand clutching a branch just below the top, and her eyes wide with fear. "Help me, Josh."

He fell to his stomach and tried to reach down for her, but she was just out of his reach and the branch she was hanging on to for dear life was already bending. It wouldn't hold for long.

She kicked her legs but couldn't find her footing.

"Hang on," Josh told her. "Hang on." He couldn't lose her like this. He just couldn't.

Miles and Lawson crouched beside him. "Grab hold of me," he told them, then dove over the side. He caught them off guard but they each grabbed a leg to keep him from falling over. He managed to slide down enough to reach her. "Take my hand," Josh told her. She was clinging to the branch like it was her lifeline but it was already starting to pull free of the dirt from her weight. "Cecile, take my hand. We'll pull you up. Trust me."

He saw hesitation on her face and it broke

him. She had no reason to trust him but she had to if she wanted to live through this. "Come on, Cecile. Don't you give up on me."

She stared up into his face, then let go of the branch and grabbed hold of his hand. He breathed a sigh of relief when she made contact. "Pull us up," he called to his brothers.

Miles and Lawson hefted them back over the edge of the cliff. Once safely on solid ground, Cecile fell into his arms. She clung to him and he held her close, his heart pounding with relief and gratefulness.

Finally, she looked up at him. "You came for me?"

"Of course, I did. You're my world. I love you, Cecile."

He expected her to smile or respond but instead she went limp. Her face paled and her eyes rolled back in her head. He patted her cheek to rouse her and only then realized his hands were covered in blood—her blood. "She's bleeding."

Paul, having experience in combat first aid, dropped to the ground beside them. He examined her wound. "She's been shot. She's going to need surgery. We have to get her out of here."

Josh held on to her as his brothers rushed to get help.

"Don't you leave me," he whispered in her ear as he lifted up prayers for her.

He'd just found the courage to admit his feelings for her. He couldn't lose her now.

The sound of beeping pulled Cecile back from the darkness. Then the pain ripped through her. She gasped and jerked awake.

Josh was instantly beside her, holding her hand. "It's okay. You're okay now," he whispered.

She lay back in the bed. "What happened?"

"You were shot in the leg. They had to perform surgery to remove the bullet. Do you remember?"

"Vaguely." Everything was coming back to her. Being abducted by Rainer. Being shot and strangled. Going over the cliff. Even the look of terror on Josh's face as he pulled her to safety. She leaned back against the pillows as she allowed the fear, anxiety and loss of hope to flow off her.

"Tom?"

"He's dead. He can't hurt you or anyone else ever again."

She sighed in relief. She'd seen him get shot

before she'd fallen but had wanted to be sure. "I can't believe I let that man get the best of me. He was right under my nose the whole time and I didn't see it."

"None of us did, but it's all over now."

Tom was dead. Erica had been found. The worst parts of her life were over and it was time to move forward. She didn't know what that meant but she hoped it included Josh—if only he could put aside his issues. Then she remembered what Tom had told her. "Josh." She reached for his hand. "Tom killed Haley."

Confusion clouded his face. "What are you talking about? Her case is nothing like the others."

"He told me he killed her. Said you came home early so he didn't have time to tie her up. She fought her way free of him, but she lost her balance and hit her head on the kitchen island."

Josh leaned back and soaked in her words. "I did come home early that night."

"I doubt we can prove it, but I did believe him when he said he was the one who did it."

He gave a long, weary sigh, then rubbed his face before taking her hand again. "I don't care about proving it. Tom Rainer is dead. That's enough justice for me. I don't care what anyone else thinks about me, Cecile, not as long as you believe in me."

"I always have."

"I know." He planted a kiss on her lips. "I love you," he told her.

She closed her eyes and soaked in his declaration of love. She'd waited so long to hear him say those words. "Are you sure, Josh?" She didn't want to doubt him but she'd already had her heart broken too often.

"I mean it. I love you, Cecile, and I don't want to lose you. Don't leave Courtland. Don't leave me."

He didn't have to worry about her leaving. "I knew the moment Rainer grabbed me that if I survived, I would never think about leaving again. This is where I want to be, Josh. My heart will always belong here in Courtland…and with you."

He leaned over and kissed her without hesitation. She touched his face and smiled. "I love you, Josh."

He grinned. "Then do something for me."

"Anything."

"Since you're going to sticking around town anyway, will you marry me? I'd really like to get started on that family we talked about."

Her heart flipped and a rush of happiness filled her. Tears pressed against her eyes. Happy tears. "Of course, I will marry you, Josh. My heart has always belonged to you."

He kissed her again and this time she knew her life was finally complete.

* * * * *

If you enjoyed this Cowboy Lawmen story by Virginia Vaughan, be sure to read the previous books in this series:

Texas Twin Abduction
Texas Holiday Hideout
Texas Target Standoff
Texas Baby Cover-Up
Texas Killer Connection

Available now from Love Inspired Suspense!

Dear Reader,

I was so excited to finally write Josh and Cecile's story! When I began this series, Cecile Richardson was only a minor character who worked with Josh. I had no idea how much I would grow to love her. She became one of those secondary characters that screamed out for a story of her own. As the series continued and she kept popping up, it became obvious how good she and Josh were together. I knew their eventual love story was going to be amazing.

So, as I wrap up my Cowboy Lawmen series, I want to thank you so much for joining me on this journey with the Avery family. I hope you've come to love them as much as I have.

Blessings,
Virginia

Get 4 FREE REWARDS!

We'll send you 2 FREE Books plus 2 FREE Mystery Gifts.

FREE
Value Over
$20

Both the **Love Inspired®** and **Love Inspired® Suspense** series feature compelling
novels filled with inspirational romance, faith, forgiveness, and hope.

YES! Please send me 2 FREE novels from the Love Inspired or Love Inspired
Suspense series and my 2 FREE gifts (gifts are worth about $10 retail). After
receiving them, if I don't wish to receive any more books, I can return the shipping
statement marked "cancel." If I don't cancel, I will receive 6 brand-new Love
Inspired Larger-Print books or Love Inspired Suspense Larger-Print books every
month and be billed just $5.99 each in the U.S. or $6.24 each in Canada. That
is a savings of at least 17% off the cover price. It's quite a bargain! Shipping
and handling is just 50¢ per book in the U.S. and $1.25 per book in Canada.*
I understand that accepting the 2 free books and gifts places me under no
obligation to buy anything. I can always return a shipment and cancel at any time.
The free books and gifts are mine to keep no matter what I decide.

Choose one: ☐ **Love Inspired**
             Larger-Print
             (122/322 IDN GNWC)

☐ **Love Inspired Suspense**
   Larger-Print
   (107/307 IDN GNWN)

Name (please print)

Address   Apt. #

City   State/Province   Zip/Postal Code

Email: Please check this box ☐ if you would like to receive newsletters and promotional emails from Harlequin Enterprises ULC and
its affiliates. You can unsubscribe anytime.

Mail to the Harlequin Reader Service:
IN U.S.A.: P.O. Box 1341, Buffalo, NY 14240-8531
IN CANADA: P.O. Box 603, Fort Erie, Ontario L2A 5X3

Want to try 2 free books from another series? Call 1-800-873-8635 or visit www.ReaderService.com.

---

*Terms and prices subject to change without notice. Prices do not include sales taxes, which will be charged (if applicable) based
on your state or country of residence. Canadian residents will be charged applicable taxes. Offer not valid in Quebec. This offer is
limited to one order per household. Books received may not be as shown. Not valid for current subscribers to the Love Inspired or
Love Inspired Suspense series. All orders subject to approval. Credit or debit balances in a customer's account(s) may be offset by
any other outstanding balance owed by or to the customer. Please allow 4 to 6 weeks for delivery. Offer available while quantities last.

Your Privacy—Your information is being collected by Harlequin Enterprises ULC, operating as Harlequin Reader Service. For a
complete summary of the information we collect, how we use this information and to whom it is disclosed, please visit our privacy notice
located at corporate.harlequin.com/privacy-notice. From time to time we may also exchange your personal information with reputable
third parties. If you wish to opt out of this sharing of your personal information, please visit readerservice.com/consumerschoice or
call 1-800-873-8635. **Notice to California Residents**—Under California law, you have specific rights to control and access your data.
For more information on these rights and how to exercise them, visit corporate.harlequin.com/california-privacy.

LIRLIS22

Get 4 FREE REWARDS!

We'll send you 2 FREE Books plus 2 FREE Mystery Gifts.

FREE
Value Over
$20

Both the **Harlequin® Special Edition** and **Harlequin® Heartwarming™** series feature compelling novels filled with stories of love and strength where the bonds of friendship, family and community unite.

YES! Please send me 2 FREE novels from the Harlequin Special Edition or Harlequin Heartwarming series and my 2 FREE gifts (gifts are worth about $10 retail). After receiving them, if I don't wish to receive any more books, I can return the shipping statement marked "cancel." If I don't cancel, I will receive 6 brand-new Harlequin Special Edition books every month and be billed just $4.99 each in the U.S or $5.74 each in Canada, a savings of at least 17% off the cover price or 4 brand-new Harlequin Heartwarming Larger-Print books every month and be billed just $5.74 each in the U.S. or $6.24 each in Canada, a savings of at least 21% off the cover price. It's quite a bargain! Shipping and handling is just 50¢ per book in the U.S. and $1.25 per book in Canada.* I understand that accepting the 2 free books and gifts places me under no obligation to buy anything. I can always return a shipment and cancel at any time. The free books and gifts are mine to keep no matter what I decide.

Choose one: ☐ **Harlequin Special Edition**
(235/335 HDN GNMP)
☐ **Harlequin Heartwarming**
Larger-Print
(161/361 HDN GNPZ)

Name (please print)

Address   Apt. #

City   State/Province   Zip/Postal Code

Email: Please check this box ☐ if you would like to receive newsletters and promotional emails from Harlequin Enterprises ULC and its affiliates. You can unsubscribe anytime.

Mail to the **Harlequin Reader Service:**
IN U.S.A.: P.O. Box 1341, Buffalo, NY 14240-8531
IN CANADA: P.O. Box 603, Fort Erie, Ontario L2A 5X3

Want to try 2 free books from another series? Call 1-800-873-8635 or visit www.ReaderService.com.

COUNTRY LEGACY COLLECTION

19 FREE BOOKS IN ALL!

Cowboys, adventure and romance await you in this new collection! Enjoy superb reading all year long with books by bestselling authors like Diana Palmer, Sasha Summers and Marie Ferrarella!